Heavens Sinners MC

Her Kinsman-Redeemer

By Darlene Tallman

Copyright

This is a work of fiction. Names, characters, places, and incidents are either the product of the author's imagination or used fictitiously, and any resemblance to actual persons, living or dead, business establishments, events or locales is entirely coincidental.

All rights reserved.

Heaven's Sinners MC – Her Kinsman-Redeemer

Copyright 2016 © Darlene Tallman

Published by: Darlene Tallman

Editor: Emily Kirkpatrick

Cover by Dark Water Covers

ALL RIGHTS RESERVED. This book contains material protected under International and Federal Copyright Laws and Treaties. Any unauthorized reprint or use of this material is prohibited. No part of this book may be reproduced or transmitted in any form or by any means, electronic or mechanical, including photocopying, recording, or by any information storage and retrieval system without express written permission from Darlene Tallman, the author / publisher.

Intended for mature audiences 18+ or older due to adult material.

Acknowledgements

You would think that after a few books, this part would get a bit easier but nope, it honestly does not. I *will* say that my beta girls were very instrumental in getting this one done timely. You see, I chose to write a story for NaNoWriMo 2016 and had "no idea" what I was going to write about. If you have no clue what NaNoWriMo is, it's a yearly contest that challenges writers and aspiring writers to put fingers to the keyboard and/or pen to paper and write 50,000 words in a month's time. Any writer will tell you that there are days when no words are written. None. At. All. Because life intrudes, day jobs intrude, illness crops up. So, to commit to do this means that you are committing to writing almost 2,000 words each and every day.

So, after saying "Sure, why not?" I was driving down the road one day with the thought of "Now what can I write?" running through my brain and a spark of an idea based on the story of Ruth and Boaz came to mind. I've always loved the story of a kinsman-redeemer, as well as the love story between Boaz and his Ruth. First things first though, I had to come up with names and my beta girls? I tossed a few out there for the female lead and they came up with the male lead's name.

As November went on, I joined in on sprints with a Facebook group I was a part of led by Cherry Shepard, NaNoWriMoFreakOut2016, and we encouraged one another (there were ninety-four of us in the group; some more vocal than others), and when I found myself unable to sleep? I knew I could find someone up and willing to sprint. So, for all my fellow "Freaks"? You were a part of this as well and I thank you.

That's when this story took on a life of its own. Several things revealed within the pages I never ever saw coming, and I found myself with watery eyes more than once. The best part? Even though the story wasn't finished, I blew through that 50k challenge and "won" NaNoWriMo 2016 for myself.

It's kind of scary taking a story I've always loved in the bible and putting the bones of that love into a contemporary romance, especially one featuring a motorcycle club (even if they are a Christian MC). Folks may think it will be "all preachy" and full of scripture and I can assure you, it is neither of those. Not because I'm ashamed of my beliefs because I am not, but because the story itself didn't call for it. There are a few places that allude to sermons I've loved over the years (one our pastor spent a year on, "I am who God says I am" was particularly revealing to our congregation as a whole), but I will never ever beat anyone over the head with my beliefs. That's not my style. There's sex and cursing in the story, not for shock effect but again, because the story went that way. I am merely the conduit for my muses. My ultimate hope is that folks see what my words were trying to convey with regards to love, the overall hope of love and how it can be redeemed by someone else.

I hope all who read the story of Zeke and Angelina, no matter how unconventional it may start, will fall in love with them. I know that my betas and I have!

Dedication

To every man and woman who has stood in front of a Sunday School class and taught about the kinsman-redeemer. And to every pastor I've ever sat up under whose teachings have given me a foundation which I draw from daily on my faith journey. Thank you for serving.

And for every man or woman who wonders – is it even possible? Yes, it *is* possible to find this type of love; I've seen it happen to so many in my life. It will be selfless, it will be kind, it will seek to serve, it will be there in the good times and the bad, the happy and the sad, and when you are old and gray and wrinkly, it will still be there. That other stuff? It's just fluff which blows away.

Table of Contents

Copyright
Acknowledgements
Dedication
Prologue
Chapter One
Chapter Two
Chapter Three
Chapter Four
Chapter Five
Chapter Six
Chapter Seven
Chapter Eight
Chapter Nine
Chapter Ten
Chapter Eleven
Chapter Twelve
Chapter Thirteen
Chapter Fourteen
Chapter Fifteen
Chapter Sixteen
Chapter Seventeen
Chapter Eighteen
Chapter Nineteen
Chapter Twenty
Chapter Twenty-one
Chapter Twenty-two
Chapter Twenty-three
Chapter Twenty-four
Epilogue
About the Author

Prologue

"Ahhh, Laser! Just like that," she moaned as she moved restlessly under the assault of his tongue and fingers. Coming undone under his caresses, she lost focus until she felt him filling her. Lifting her face, she brought him closer and mimicked his movements with her mouth against his.

Finally spent, he collapsed to the side of her and they struggled to catch their breath. "Love you, 'Lina."

"Love you too, Laser," she whispered.

"C'mon, let's get cleaned up and get some sleep, yeah?"

"Mm-kay, but I want it on record I'm perfectly content to stay right here!"

One shower later and they were back in bed, cuddled close and quietly talking. He knew she'd been worried about her courses at the local college and he worked to soothe her. She loved that after all their years together, he just got her and knew what to say and do to calm her nerves.

She drifted off to sleep with his whispered words in her ear.

***

Waking up, she found herself cold only that couldn't be right. She could feel his arm laying heavy across her waist and his chest against her back. Reaching out, she grasped his hand which is under her breast and found it icy. As fear touched her heart, she rolled over, softly saying, "Laser? Honey? Why are you so cold?" One glance at his face and she knew.

Keening wails brought Dex to their door at the clubhouse. "Angelina? ANGELINA! What's going on? I'm coming in!"

As Dex broke down the door, she was crouched over Laser, crying and pleading for him to wake up. Reaching the bed, Dex could see that Laser wouldn't be waking up and that his old lady was going into shock. Calling out, he wasn't surprised to see Renda, his old lady, come up alongside him and then crawl onto the bed to pull Angelina into her arms as she wrapped her in the blankets. Several more of the Brothers came in and a decision was made to call an ambulance. Sadness permeated the room. Laser was one of the founding members and he was held in high regard by his Brothers.

***

Hearing a knock on the door, she called out, "Come in" and smiled wanly when she saw Dex and Renda. "I'm almost ready to go," she told them, applying a little lip gloss. No sense in a lot of eye makeup, all the claims of being waterproof could not hold up against the onslaught of tears that constantly overtook her.

"Wanted to talk to you for a minute," Dex finally said.

"Oh…okay," she mumbled, finishing and coming to sit on the edge of the bed.

"Listen, I know this has been a helluva shock to all of us, especially you. I've known Laser all my life and we played sports in school and everything. None of us had any clue he had that condition, Angel, but I pray you heard the doctor say that there was nothing that could have been done and that he went painlessly, yeah?"

She looked at Dex and nodded. "I...I just don't know what I should do now," she finally stammered out.

"What do you mean, darlin'?"

"Well, I mean, with him gone and all, he *was* my home. You know what I came out of and there's nothing for me there."

Renda finally spoke up, saying, "Sweetie, you have a home here with the Heaven's Sinners as long as you draw breath. That doesn't change just because your old man died. Since you're in school, you need to stay and finish-Laser would want you to finish. When you're done, if the memories are too much, we have another chapter up in North Georgia in the mountains."

"But I need to work now that he's gone."

Dex interrupted saying, "No, actually you don't, darlin', because you'll still get Laser's cut even though he's gone since you're his old lady. You've got a place to live, keep in school. We've got your back and you know that, right?"

"Yeah, Dex, I do. Honestly, without y'all, I don't know that I would still be breathing," she finally said.

Dex looked down at the woman his Brother called Lina. Petite and curvy with thick strawberry-blonde hair, she captured his Brother's attention the first time they saw her trying to steal food. From that moment on, Laser had made it his mission to find out everything he could about her and then bring her into the fold as his old lady. He knew that if his Brother had one regret, it would be that they hadn't ever made it legal, but she had proven time and again that she was old lady material. He hoped that she healed from losing Laser because she'd make some lucky man a good old lady when she was ready again.

"C'mon, Angel, the pastor is here and ready to get the memorial started, yeah?" he finally said, coaxing both women from the room.

***

Six weeks later

Blowing out a breath, Angelina looked at the stick again. While she was happy that she'd have something to remember him by, the fact that she was going to be a single mom was a daunting prospect. *You're not alone, my Daughter* whispered across her soul.

Chapter One

Three years later

"Congratulations Class of 2016!" the Dean said through the cheers and air horns. "Now go and be a light."

Smiling at a few of the friends she made, she hurried to the group of men and women wearing the Heaven's Sinners cuts and to the double stroller that Renda was pushing. Leaning down, she kissed each little sleeping head, amazed that they could sleep through the deafening noise. Standing back up, she was engulfed in a set of muscular arms and could hear Dex's voice as he said, "Congrats, Angel. Laser would be so proud of you for pushing through and finishing!"

The tears didn't come as often or as easy as they did when he first died and she said a silent prayer of thanks. Being pregnant and grieving at the same time had her hormones going nuts and she was grateful that his Brothers and the old ladies understood and provided her the safety net she needed whenever life was "too much" to deal with. But at the mention of his name and thinking of how far she had come while by his side, a few silently trickled down her face.

"Ah, no tears now, darlin', today's a good day, yeah?" Dex asked.

"It is, Dex. It is. Was just thinking about how proud he would be that I *did* finish and how sad it makes me that the girls will never know their daddy."

"Darlin', I know you'll tell them all about their daddy. Just remember something, yeah? You don't have to be alone the rest of your life. Laser wouldn't have wanted that for you or those girls."

"Yeah, I know, but honestly? As busy as these past few years have been, that's not been a priority in my life. Not for nothing, but it will take a pretty special man who has no problem raising someone else's kids and who will understand that Laser will always hold a place in my heart. Y'all rescued me all those years ago and I don't want to think about what would have become of me if you hadn't found me when you did."

Dex thought back to the day Angelina came into their lives. They had been in a store and seen her attempting to steal food. She was unkempt and so thin it was obvious she was on the verge of starvation. To keep her from being arrested, Laser had stepped up and offered to buy her dinner. They hadn't had an easy time of it in the beginning-she was mistrustful of them and their motives, having come from a foster home where lies and manipulation were praised and her honest, hard-working nature was sneered at. She was even more hesitant when she realized that most of the members attended the local interfaith church because "the church" had hurt her badly. He recalled it had taken Laser a good six months before she trusted him enough to become his old lady and after that they were pretty much attached at the hip. He had watched her bloom into a beautiful young woman alongside his best friend, and saw how she embraced the redemption that was preached in their church. Even though he and Laser were the same age, he sometimes felt fatherly toward the young woman-something she wouldn't want to know.

"God had a bigger plan for you, Angel, and He still does," Dex finally said. "Now, enough of this serious stuff, let's head back to the clubhouse because you've earned this party!"

She grinned and linked her arm in his and followed him and Renda to the SUV the club had gotten her when they found out she was having twins. She truly was blessed. She knew that there were clubs out there that would have kicked her to the curb when her old man passed away, but the Heaven's Sinners maintained she was part of the family and each of them helped her get to this point.

Arriving at the clubhouse, she and Renda got the girls out of the SUV and headed in where there was a huge banner saying "Congrats Angel – Class of 2016!" hanging over the bar. A table off to the side had food and a huge cake and another table was covered in gift bags. "C'mon girl, let's eat!" Renda said, watching her friend stand there with her mouth hanging open. Brothers and their old ladies came by for hugs, congratulating her and kissing her. It truly was a family atmosphere and once again, she was hit with a pang of longing wishing that Laser had been there as well.

Chapter Two

Zeke huffed in frustration. He knew from looking over the books that their former accountant had been embezzling from the club's businesses, but he couldn't figure out how much or where it went. Thankfully, when it had become obvious, they had the man arrested and he was currently awaiting trial, but that didn't help him figure anything out. He needed help and wasn't sure where it was coming from, but he needed it yesterday. Hearing the door open, he looked up and saw Preacher step into the room.

"Hey, Brother, what's going on?" he asked.

"Eh, not a whole lot. Is your phone on?"

"Yeah, why?"

"Well, Dex has been trying to reach you and when he got your voicemail multiple times in a row, he called me. I think we may have a solution to our accountant problem."

Sitting back in his chair, he motioned for Preacher to take a seat and continue.

"Seems that there's an old lady whose old man died that just got her degree in accounting. She has been doing the books for the South Georgia chapter's businesses for years now. She's got her licenses or certificates or whatever the hell she has to have and has expressed to Dex that now that she's graduated, she'd like to relocate."

He thought for a minute before replying, "Wasn't that Laser's old lady?"

"Yeah, Angelina. She's got two little girls that are Laser's, but the town doesn't hold anything else for her other than her relationship with Dex and Renda and the other Heavens Sinner's members. All the memories must make it hard."

Thinking out loud, he said, "Well, we have the cottage off Main Street, it needs cleaning and a good painting, but it would give her somewhere to live. With her having kids, do you think she'd be able to handle the books for the businesses?"

Preacher looked at him before he answered. "Yeah, you know a lot of that stuff can be done online now, so we could set up one of the rooms as an office for her. From what I gather talking to Dex, she's pretty hands-on with her daughters and won't want to leave them with strangers."

"Alright, what do we have to lose? We'll go ahead and mention it in Church so everyone knows what is happening and see if any of the Brothers and old ladies can help us get the house ready for its new resident."

Preacher smiled inside. He knew his Brother didn't remember the woman from their visits to South Georgia, but he had an inkling that she was going to blow Zeke's socks off. Ever since Gayla took off and left him with their son, Thad, Zeke hadn't shown any lasting interest in anyone. He had kept anything casual, and for one reason only. He knew from talking with Dex that Angelina had focused her energies on college, grieving, and her girls, and that he and Renda felt she was ready to get back to living again.

***

"But Dex, I'm happy here!" Angelina said. "I don't know anyone in our North Georgia chapter!"

"Darlin', you've met them during runs and meet-ups," he patiently reminded her. "And Zeke has need of a grade-A accountant because his was caught with his hands in the cookie jar."

"Can't he just go to Accountants R Us?" she replied in a snarky tone.

"Now, now, you know that's not how it's done. They've got a house for you and the girls already, and you'll be making a good salary with benefits."

"What about daycare for the girls? You know I don't like leaving them," she protested.

"They've set up an office in the house so you can work from home, darlin', and whenever you have to meet with Zeke, you can either take them with you or one of the old ladies can keep the girls."

"Well, the only way I'll go is if you take the money you've been giving me for Laser's cut and put it into a trust for the girls. Since I'll be earning a salary, I can pay my own way," she finally told him.

He grinned at her and she knew it was pretty much a done deal. "Do they have a church up there like we've got here?" she asked.

"Yeah, darlin', they do. We're accepted up there just like here so you won't have to worry about that," he told her.

"How soon?" she asked, interrupting his thoughts.

"He needed someone yesterday, but I figured a week," he replied.

She looked around the house and he could already see her thinking about what needed to be done. "Darlin', it's a fresh start for you and the girls. Maybe you should take it as such and only take your clothes and their toys and the things that are special to you. Leave the furniture and stuff."

She looked at him. He knew her so well. "I think I like that idea," she softly said. "It's hard to see 'our stuff' every day and know that he's not coming home."

"Then it's settled. I'll get some of the old ladies over here with some boxes so you can get started, and give Zeke a call letting him know you'll be up there by next Saturday."

Holy smokes! A week? With a small sigh she smiled and asked, "What about your books?"

"Oh darlin', not to worry. Since everything is online, we're still using you. It will give me and

Renda a reason to visit you and those sweet girls."

She laughed and he marveled at the sound. She hadn't had a whole lot of joy in the past few years and hearing the almost-musical sound of her laughter gave him the confirmation he needed that this was going to be a good thing for her.

Chapter Three

Zeke went through the house one more time to make sure that everything was as ready for its new inhabitants as it could be. One of the bedrooms had been set up for the two little girls, who he had learned were three, and the old ladies had outdone themselves, a pale pink coated the walls and each twin-sized bed had a princess canopy over it. Pictures had been hung and each bed had a Cabbage Patch doll sitting waiting on it, gifts from the members' kids.

Striding back down the hall, he entered the master bedroom and looked at it with a clinical eye. Light hardwood flooring, sage green walls, and an antique white wrought iron queen-sized bed took center stage. Off to the right was a small sitting area where they had placed a chaise lounge, a table and lamp, and a television. The left side of the room had two doors; a massive walk-in closet that any woman would drool over, and an en suite bathroom that sported a walk-in shower as well as a Jacuzzi tub. Leaving the master bedroom, he went back down the hall and into the office. Bookshelves lined one wall and they had managed to find an L-shaped desk. Dex had sent him the information for the computers and his IT guy had made sure that the set-up would be compatible with the South Georgia chapter since she would be handling the books for both chapters.

He still couldn't remember the woman, but he trusted his VP and he trusted Dex, so he was going to roll with it. Hearing a noise outside, he made his way out to the front porch and saw an SUV pulling in alongside a U-Haul truck. *Damn* he thought. Dex had indicated she was leaving her furniture so what on earth could she have needed a U-Haul for? Heading down the stairs, he stopped short seeing the petite redhead step out of the SUV and stretch. Something deep inside creaked open and for a minute, he fancied it was the gate he had around his heart. Shaking his head at his nonsensical thoughts, he called out, "Hello! Glad to see you didn't have any problems finding the place."

She looked up and he was hit by the clear green eyes that stared at him. She didn't say anything at first and he worried that this wasn't going to be a good idea, until she smiled and replied, "Hi. I think I am running a bit late but Dex insisted he and Renda come along so they could bring some of the girls' outside toys."

Ah, so that's what was in the U-Haul he thought. Walking over to where Dex had stopped, he man-hugged him and kissed Renda's cheek before saying, "How much is in the U-Haul?"

Dex shot Renda a look and started laughing, saying, "Well, my old lady convinced Angel that it would be easier to buy the stuff she needed *before* she got here, so they shopped for what she needed and then packed it up. Mostly kitchen things, but she also got towels and whatnot. The guys and I got the girls a swing set for up here and that's in there as well."

"Well, some of my guys will be here shortly and we should be able to get it unpacked and put up so she can get settled in quickly," Zeke finally said.

✳✳✳

Holy shit! He was a mighty fine specimen of a man she thought as she worked to get the girls out of the car. They had been good on the trip but she knew it had taken a lot out of them being cooped up in their seats for hours on end. Even having Renda occasionally switch over as a passenger had gotten old and they were a bit cranky and out of sorts. She was hoping that she could put them down for a nap for a little bit to give them all a break. When she finally got both sleeping girls in her arms, she made her way over to the man who was going to be her new boss.

"I...I'm Angelina Jones," she said, trying to hold out her hand.

He looked down at the tiny woman standing in front of him and catalogued everything he could see without even thinking: petite, strawberry-blonde hair pulled up in a ponytail, green eyes, a smattering of freckles across the bridge of her nose, and a light floral scent that teased his senses. "I'm Zeke Morgan. C'mon in and I'll show you around."

"Okay. Um, I need to lay the girls down for a nap."

"Not a problem. Their room is already set up."

Already set up? Out loud she said, "Really? I was planning to shop for furniture once we got up here and was just going to use an air mattress until it came."

"We took care of the bedrooms and a basic kitchen table, you'll still have to get living room furniture and that kind of thing, but the old ladies wanted to make sure you and your kids would have someplace to sleep when you got here."

"That was very kind of them," she replied as she tried to juggle both sleeping girls.

Seeing her struggle, he reached out and said, "May I?" as he took one of the little girls from her.

"Thank you," she said, smiling gratefully. "They tend to be dead weight when they're sleeping!"

He chuckled. "I remember that from when my son was younger."

Damn. He was married. Wait, where did that come from? There was no time for a man, not with two toddlers and a new job!

"How old is your son?" she asked.

"He just turned sixteen, but I swear he tries to act older than me sometimes," he replied as he led her into the house.

"I'm sure he keeps you and your wife on your toes."

"It's just us. His mom is dead."

"Oh, I'm so sorry!" *Way to stick your foot in your mouth* she thought.

He stopped and turned to look at her and could see the distress written on her face. She wouldn't make a good poker player as every thought was evident. "Hey, it happened a long time ago. She left us when he was a little older than your girls, and died a year or two after that. He doesn't remember anything different, but has been blessed with an abundance of aunts thanks to the old ladies up here, as well as a grandmother who dotes on him."

"I'm glad you had that for him. The girls have Dex and of course, all the Brothers, so I've had to work hard to make sure they don't turn into little divas. Hasn't been easy, that's for sure!"

Looking down at the little girl who was sleeping against his chest, he could understand why his southern Brothers spoiled them. They both had strawberry blonde hair like their mother and a smattering of freckles crossed the bridge of this one's nose. Glancing at Angelina's bundle, he could see the same on that little one and wondered how she told them apart. "How do you tell them apart?" he finally asked.

"Well, they're pretty much identical except for their eye color. You're holding Melora and her eyes are green like mine. Cailyn has gray eyes. I'm sure they'll still attempt the typical twin switching because most folks won't notice that little detail right away, but hopefully not."

Reaching the girls' bedroom, he shifted to allow her to go through the door first and heard her gasp of pleasure at seeing how the room was decorated. "Oh, Zeke, they're going to be over the moon when they wake up! This is too much, y'all shouldn't have gone to so much trouble!"

Carefully laying Melora down and covering her with the throw at the end of the bed, he turned and looked at Angelina. "Angelina, look at me, please."

Inwardly she gulped. She recognized the "President" tone in his voice and wondered what she could have done already to earn that tone of voice. "Yes?" she answered shakily.

"You and your girls are part of the Heaven's Sinner family. Family takes care of one another and that's what we are doing for the three of you. It was no trouble and no bother, y'hear? The old ladies truly enjoyed being able to do this and honestly, Preacher's wife had to be corralled because she was ready to outfit the whole house. Both Preacher and I had to tell her that you would probably like some input."

"Thank you. When can I meet the old ladies so I can thank them?"

Gracious. He could hear it in her tone and see it in the manner she held herself. Most women would have been beside themselves upset because someone else made choices for them. Yet here she was, uprooted from the only family she knew and thrust in the middle of another chapter, and instead of being upset that they had decorated her daughters' room, she was thankful. "Soon. We generally do a potluck meal every Sunday after church. I know you just got here, but hopefully, with the help of the Brothers who are coming shortly, we can get you mostly settled. And I'm sure those Brothers will bring their old ladies, so you'll likely meet a lot of them today as well."

"I look forward to it. Thank you again for letting me relocate."

"You're welcome. Dex said you know your stuff and I'm hoping you'll be able to help me figure out where it went. The books are a mess-I know you aren't actually starting until next week, but maybe tomorrow while we are relaxing after church I can give you the information you need to get started?"

"That sounds like a plan to me."

Hearing the unmistakable noise of a lot of bikes, he headed back outside. Seeing his Brothers and old ladies pulling in made his heart swell. They truly were the hands and feet of Christ, and the fact that they made themselves available to help someone new to their chapter was inspiring. As he reached the group, he saw Dex going around thanking them for helping Angelina get settled. He knew from talking to Dex that he felt almost fatherly toward her even though he was the same age as her old man. The thought ran through his head that fatherly wasn't exactly how he felt and he mentally shook himself-he was content to be single and raise Thad to be the man God wanted him to be.

"Angel? Come over here, Zeke and I want to introduce you to some of the Brothers and their old ladies," Dex called out.

As she went over to stand by Dex and Zeke, her first thought was *wow* because every one of the men and their old ladies radiated the love of Jesus. Names passed in a blur and she knew it would take a while for her to put them with the faces. Zeke quickly got the men started bringing in the boxes and the next thing she knew, she had six old ladies in her kitchen helping her unpack, wash and put away the dishes and whatnot. Renda directed the men with the other boxes, and she and several of the other old ladies got the bathrooms set up and her clothes put away.

Several hours later, she smelled burgers cooking and looked outside to see Dex manning a grill. *Wait a minute, I don't have a grill* she thought. Heading out the back door she stopped up short. The backyard was already fenced and there was a new swing set and playhouse set off to the side for the girls, there was a patio set on the deck and one of the biggest grills she had ever seen. "Uh, Dex? I don't remember owning any of this stuff," she said after looking around for a few minutes.

"Angel, it's a housewarming gift from the Brothers," he told her as he expertly flipped the burgers. "Renda and Preacher's old lady went to pick up the sides for the burgers. Gotta feed everyone sweetheart."

Overwhelmed. That word ran through her mind as she looked around again and then looked back into the house. Very few boxes remained to be unpacked and they were mostly knick-knacks, pictures and books, which she could handle on her own. She was pretty much settled other than going to the grocery store to stock up. Going over to Dex, she gave him a quick hug in thanks and headed back into the house so she could see if the girls were up yet and jot down a list. She would need to ask one of the old ladies where the closest store was so she could take care of that tomorrow after church and the potluck at the clubhouse.

***

"Hey sweet girls! Did you sleep okay?" she asked as she entered their bedroom. Thankfully, despite the noise of so many people in and out of the house, they had slept without disruption. Trying to keep them on a schedule these past two days hadn't been easy, but she had done it.

"Momma?" Melora called.

"Yes, honey-girl."

"Our room?"

"Yes, it's your room, do you like it? Some very nice people made sure that you would know you are princesses," she told them both. "Now, who has to potty?" Both girls jumped out of their beds with their new babies in their arms and came to her for hugs.

Cailyn, the quieter of the two, motioned to be picked up. New places sometimes scared her and Angelina made a mental note to keep her with either Dex, Renda or herself until she got used to this new group of people. Walking into their bathroom-she was thrilled that each bedroom had its own bathroom, it would make life easier-she saw that they had apparently modified it. There was a double sink vanity, two toilets, and a huge bathtub along with a shower. She helped both girls wash up once they were finished, and smiled at the fact that there were two little stepstools in front of the sink for them to reach it. Someone had taken a lot of care to make sure they would be comfortable and she was grateful for that fact.

Taking each girl by the hand, she walked back out onto the deck. Seeing Dex, they dropped her hands and ran over to him calling out, "Unka Dex, Unca Dex!" He stepped back from the grill and crouched down so he could pick both girls up and give them kisses, something they loved judging by their giggles.

"You girls want to see what your uncles got you?" he asked.

"Yes please," they said.

He walked down the back stairs and on over to the playhouse. If the squeals of delight at the miniature house were any indication, she was going to be outside. A lot. *Oh well, they made pretty strong sunblock these days* she thought. She reached the playhouse and stopped, amazement written over her face. It looked like they had bought one of those mini-buildings and then decorated it inside for two little girls to play house and dolls. Already, Melora was at the 'kitchen' cooking something like her 'Unka Dex' which was a sight to behold.

"Dex…I don't know what to say! What…how did you get this here?"

"It was delivered a little while ago while you and the old ladies were working in the house."

"Dex, it's too much!"

"Angel, you know we look out for family. This is your time to shine with those babies and we wanted to make sure you were set up to do that," he responded.

Realizing that she wasn't going to get through to him, she left him in charge of the girls and carried the burgers into the house. Once she hunted down her purse, she grabbed her grocery list pad and started writing things down. She had brought some of the non-perishable items, but would have to get the basics: eggs, milk, bread, lunch meat. Opening the refrigerator to see if there was an egg container, she gasped. It was full of all the condiments and basics that she had on her list, along with a bottle of wine and a note that said "Welcome to Heaven's Sinners – North Georgia" and it was signed "Heaven's Sinners Old Ladies" with a list of names and phone numbers and instructions to add them to her phone! *Holy shit* she thought. Checking the pantry, she was again blown away because there were cereals that the girls liked, as well as soups and even stuff for spaghetti. Hearing voices, she turned and saw Renda and the woman she presumed was Preacher's old lady walking in the door with several bags, with a prospect coming in behind them loaded down.

"Renda! Did you buy out the store?" she asked.

Renda started laughing. "No, sweetheart. I picked up some things I know you and the girls like, and the rest is for everyone who helped today. Did Dex get the burgers done?"

"Yeah, I just brought them in," she replied as she started putting the items away. Looking at Renda, she softly said, "I'm kind of speechless right now. This is far more than I ever expected."

The other woman said, "Hi, I'm Preacher's old lady, Eva. We wanted to welcome you and your girls North Georgia style so you would know how happy we are that you're here."

"Thank you, Eva. I'm positively blown away by all of this and don't even know what to say!"

"You just said it, Angelina. You're family and we take care of our family, especially when they're making a new start. Since we know that Zeke is eager to turn the books over to you, we knew it would be a challenge to set up house *and* start a new job and we wanted to make it easier on you."

"Y'all definitely did that," she replied softly.

"Where are the girls?" Renda asked.

"They're outside with Dex in their playhouse. Did you know about that?"

Renda grinned. "Yeah, babe, I knew about it. Hell, the girls and I picked it out and you better be glad because even as big as your backyard is, I don't think you would have been thrilled to have the one the guys were gunning for!"

Angelina laughed. The Brothers all had a "go big or go home" philosophy in just about everything they did-from runs to rallys to family outings- and she had been on the receiving end of their generosity countless times since Laser had died. "Thank you all for tempering their enthusiasm. I love them all, but they can get over the top sometimes, y'know?"

At that, Eva began laughing and said, "Ah, seems that our guys are the same way. They don't meet a stranger and I cannot tell you how many pies they have their fingers in around town to ensure that those less fortunate know God's love."

"I'm looking forward to getting involved with things Eva, once I get a handle on what Zeke wants me to do," Angelina said.

"Oh honey, you'll be involved, that's for sure! Did Zeke mention we do a potluck on Sundays after church? Just a family day with all the kids, no talk of work or anything like that. Sometimes, we'll have dance off parties with everyone."

"I think I'm going to like it here. Heaven's Sinners saved me long ago and I'll be happy to pay it forward any way I can."

Eva looked at the petite redhead and could tell there was a story there. She walked over to the young woman and put her arms around her shoulders and softly said, "I'm happy to listen whenever you want to talk."

Angelina looked at her in astonishment before replying, "Okay. I'd like that very much."

More noise at the back door had the three women looking to see Dex coming in with the two girls, Zeke and the rest of the Brothers and old ladies trailing behind. Walking up to Renda, Dex gave her a quick kiss before he asked Zeke to bless the food so they could eat. With every head bowed, Zeke gave thanks for the hands that had helped today and for the food they were about to eat.

As talking and laughter filled the air, she went and made plates for the girls who were working on charming their way through the group of people. Several of the old ladies came up to her and told her that they had kids in the same age range and she was excited about the fact that they would get some socialization.

✱✱✱

With the meal cleaned up and almost everyone gone save Dex and Renda, who were staying overnight, and Zeke, they settled at the kitchen table. The girls, still a bit tired from their moving adventure, went down without a fight, leaving the adults to talk.

"Angelina, here's the address for the church and also for the clubhouse," Zeke said.

Taking the paper and noticing the strong, bold pen strokes, she said, "Thank you. For everything. I am blown away, quite honestly."

He looked at her and again felt *something* inside. Deciding that he would pray about it once he was home and alone, he said, "Well, there's more."

"Uh, what do you mean 'there's more'?" she questioned.

"Since we didn't know what kind of living room furniture you wanted, we set up an account at the furniture store in town. You go shopping on Monday and get what you want and need."

"But…but I thought I was starting work on Monday?" she asked.

"Tuesday's soon enough," he replied. "They've been a hot mess for months now and one more day isn't going to make a difference."

"Okay, if you're sure?" she asked.

"Positive."

Renda looked at Dex and he rolled his eyes before bursting into laughter. "Guess we aren't going home tomorrow afternoon after all, huh?" he asked, teasing his wife.

"Uh, no. I'm going shopping with Angelina while you and Zeke do whatever you Presidents do when you get together."

Angelina sat there stunned. Her mind went back to when Laser and Dex first found her and she thought about how different her life could have been if they had walked on by instead of stepping in and stopping her. "Dex? Seems to me that Heaven's Sinners has been saving me for years now," she softly said. "And if I've never said it before I'm saying it now, thank you. I don't know where I would have ended up if y'all hadn't stepped in that day."

"Darlin', there was no way I could have or would have stopped him. Even then, you had the look of someone who was going to have a great purpose and that wouldn't have been served in an orange jumpsuit."

Zeke looked between the two of them knowing he didn't have the full story but realizing that he had gotten enough to know that somehow, Dex and Laser had interceded on her behalf. While he was curious as to what had happened, he knew that if she wanted to share she would in her own time. Standing up, he looked at the three of them and said, "I'm heading out. Look forward to seeing y'all in the morning."

Angelina stood and walked with him to the door. As he turned, she lightly touched his arm to catch his attention and when he looked at her, she looked up and said, "Thank you again for all you and the North Georgia chapter have done to make this move so easy for the girls and I. You'll never know how much it means to me."

Looking down at her and seeing the sincerity shining from her eyes, he took a quick breath in before replying, "You're more than welcome. See you tomorrow."

Chapter Four

Angelina woke up with a start before she realized that she was in her new room in her new house. She still couldn't believe the changes in her life, not just in the past week but over the past six years. From homeless to having a home with two healthy, beautiful girls and a family that was unlike any other. She took a few minutes to thank God knowing that at any minute she would need to get up and start getting herself ready to go before she got the girls up. She was grateful for the pastor from her old church, the foster home she had been in was all about keeping up appearances and it had left her confused about the hypocritical nature of people and somewhat bitter against the church. When he explained that there were those out there who had missed what it meant with respect to the redemptive nature of the work on the Cross, she understood that they had not ever truly accepted that gift. It was then and only then that she was finally able to shed the shame and guilt over things outside of her control and begin building a new belief tree about herself-she was beloved, she had worth and was worthy of love. Through it all, Laser had been at her side.

She smiled in remembrance of him. He was so vibrant and larger than life and despite his own screwed up past, he had loved her to the best of his ability. She never understood why they hadn't gotten married, something that had saddened her in the beginning because at least then, she would have had something of "his" attached to her. Then she found out she was pregnant and realized that she had a piece of him that would live on through their child. When she found out she was carrying twins, her joy knew no bounds despite realizing that it would be challenging to be a single mom with not one child but two. However, her family had come up alongside her and walked her through it every step of the way. Her church from before would have shunned her for being an "unwed mother" but the church she attended with the rest of the folks at Heaven's Sinner MC had showered her with love and gifts. Looking at her phone, she realized she needed to get up and get a move on. Eva had told her the day before to dress for comfort; the church didn't thrive on ceremony and there were people who would be there in suits and dresses while others would be in jeans. The Brothers would, of course, have their cuts on but they'd have a dress shirt underneath.

***

Heading into the kitchen with the girls, she saw that Renda was pulling a pan out of the oven. "What's that?" she asked.

"Well, I didn't think about it last night, so I had Dex run out and get the stuff for you to make your brownies. This is the second pan and I already put the mint topping on the first pan. That way, we have something to take to the clubhouse for the potluck."

"Oh, shit, I never thought about that at all!"

"No worries, I've got you covered and honestly, they probably wouldn't have thought about it being that you just moved in yesterday. Now, let's get those girls fed so we'll be ready to head out, okay?"

Feeding the girls was sometimes an exercise in futility, but thankfully today, they were cooperative. As they ate, the adults talked some more about the changes and Angelina expressed her thanks once again to her friends.

"Angel, no thanks are necessary," Dex told her firmly.

"Actually, they are Dex," she replied. "If I grow complacent thanking people when they do something for me, I'll be no better than those who feel entitled to every little thing. I don't take what was done for the girls and I for granted or lightly."

"And we all know that, sweetie, hell, even the old ladies from this chapter remarked on how gracious they thought you were," Renda said.

"They seem like a great group of women and I can't wait to get to know them better. Several have kids the same age as the girls, or close enough to it, that I know they'll have some socialization."

"Don't forget that they have a daycare too, darlin', and that will help on the days when you have to make your rounds."

"Yeah, just like I did back home. I figure that Zeke and I will go over some of that today and hopefully, on Tuesday, he will take me around to the businesses so I can meet everyone and get the paperwork I need to get started."

"You're in good hands with him. He's good people, Angel, or I wouldn't have suggested you to him or even considered letting you relocate."

She thought cautiously about what she was going to say next. "Um, he seems nice enough…" she started.

"Sweetie, he's a handsome, godly *biker* for heaven's sake!" cried Renda.

"But Renda, that's just…I don't know, I mean, I've had an old man, remember? There's no way…"

Dex, realizing that he was likely impeding the talk, said, "C'mon girls, let's go get cleaned up and let your momma and aunt Renda talk, okay?"

Once they had left the room, Angelina looked at Renda and voiced her concerns. "I mean, wouldn't it be weird if I got involved with him? Hell, we literally *just met* yesterday and while I admit that I felt an attraction, you know me well enough to know that I am not a pursuer by nature."

"Sweetie, haven't you ever heard the story of Ruth?"

"Well yeah, she followed her mother-in-law Naomi to Naomi's homeland."

"And…?"

"And what?"

"There was more to the story. Boaz was a distant relation and Naomi had Ruth follow him in the fields and he allowed some of the best stuff to be left for her to gather *and* he eventually took her as his wife as the kinsman-redeemer."

"Hmm. I don't recall that part. I guess I better reread that book, huh? Anyhow, we're getting ahead of ourselves totally. How about I work on getting settled in here and whatever happens, happens?"

"Look, you're young and have your whole life ahead of you, sweetie. All I'm going to say is don't shut the door on something if it presents itself."

"Okay, okay. I won't, I promise!"

Chapter Five

He found himself standing outside of church and told himself he was waiting for Dex, even though he kind of suspected he was lying to himself. There was something captivating about the woman he had met yesterday and even though he had prayed last night, he was no closer to receiving any kind of revelation or confirmation. He saw the SUV pull into the parking lot and made his way over to where Dex was pulling in, going to the side where Angelina was sitting and opening the door once the car was shut off.

"Good morning, Angelina. I trust you and the girls had a good first night?" he asked her.

"Good morning, Zeke. Yes, as a matter of fact, we were very comfortable. And whoever decided to expand the girls' bathroom like they did is an absolute saint!"

He chuckled before saying, "Well, I'm no saint, but I remember a friend once having twins remarking that the best thing they ever did was build out their bathroom like that and I guess it stuck with me so when I heard you had twins, I had the guys do the same."

"Thank you. It's much appreciated, that's for sure!"

As they made their way into the church, he guided her toward the nursery where she filled out paperwork and got a restaurant-style beeper that the workers informed her would vibrate if there was a reason she was needed. "What a neat system this is," she said.

"It keeps the interruptions to a minimum even though Pastor says he doesn't notice it too much," the woman said.

Leaning down, she kissed both girls saying, "Have fun and be sweet my babies."

Walking into the sanctuary, she was amazed at the number of Heaven's Sinners cuts she saw. They took up almost a third of the sanctuary and she was greeted by those who had been at the house the day before with a wave or a nod or a smile. Smiling back, she continued to follow Zeke, sliding in next to Renda while he sat next to her on the other side, handing her a bulletin.

***

If she had to use one word to describe how she felt after the service it would be refreshed. The Pastor had started a new series entitled "I am who God says I am" and judging by what he had covered this morning, she was going to get a lot out of it.

As they made their way back to the SUV with Zeke once again helping her with the girls, she looked up at him and said, "I think I'm going to like it here."

"I'm glad. We're involved in a lot of community things, both as the MC as well as part of this church, and I'm sure you'll find something that sparks your interest," he told her as he buckled Cailyn into her carseat.

Looking over at Dex, he asked, "Do you remember how to get to the clubhouse?"

"Yeah, Brother, we'll see you there. Going to stop and grab a few things."

"No need, we have it under control."

"Ah, I forgot to grab more pull-ups," Angelina admitted.

"I'm sure we have those as well."

"I'll need them for later too."

"In that case, we will see you there, okay?"

"Thank you."

***

What a gorgeous day for a potluck she thought, looking around at the families and kids surrounding the back section of the property. The brownies had been well-received and the food was wonderful-all the comfort foods one could want. Now, the older kids were off playing tag while the younger ones were on the playset that was over under some shade trees.

As she headed over to grab a drink, she ran into Eva. "Hey girl, those brownies were a hit! You know you'll have to bring them every week now, right?"

Angelina laughed and said, "That's fine. I don't mind making something else as well. What about a potato salad? I've heard mine is pretty good."

"I suspect anything you make will be well-received. C'mon, I want to introduce you to more of the old ladies. These are the ones who weren't there yesterday, but they all helped get the house ready in some way."

"Oh, I've been wanting to meet them! I don't promise to remember all their names yet, but want to thank everyone for what they did to help get the house ready."

Eva walked with her over to the group of women who were sitting near the play area and said, "Everyone, this is Angelina and those two cuties out on the playground are her little girls."

With "hellos" and "welcomes" ringing in her ears, she did her best to remember the names but they started to blur together. Laughing, she raised her hands and said, "I can promise I won't remember your names right now. Faces? Absolutely. But names sometimes take me a bit longer, so bear with me as I commit them all to memory. I wanted to thank all of you for everything you and your old men did to help get the house ready for the girls and I. It's absolutely gorgeous and I love the colors you chose and the girls were over the moon when they saw their room. Whoever had the idea to get them new "babies" is also to be commended because they haven't let them out of their sight since they laid eyes on them."

One woman, who introduced herself as Marta, said, "We're glad you're here Angelina. Anything you need, you let us know and we'll help you get it, okay?"

"I appreciate that greatly. I do need to know where the local grocery store is because there are a few things the girls like in particular and I need to get them."

Eva looked over at Renda and said, "If you don't mind me tagging along tomorrow on your furniture shopping trip, I'll be glad to show you some of the local area. And we put a list of the local pediatrician and pharmacy, as well as a few other important numbers, on the side of your refrigerator. I forgot to show you yesterday."

"Oh that's awesome! I didn't even look because the girls were wiped out and we were too. Honestly, without all the extra hands yesterday, I would probably be more tired than I am."

"Many hands makes light the work," said one of the women. Debra? Deanna? No matter, she'd learn their names in time.

"I fully agree."

She sat there in the company of mostly strangers, save Renda, and felt more comfortable than she had in years. They talked about the upcoming MC events, as well as things happening at church that they wanted to get involved in and she listened, taking mental notes.

"Eva? Do they have a woman's Sunday school class?" she finally asked during a lull in the conversation.

"They do. I think they're getting ready to start a Beth Moore study. I can find out for you if you're interested?"

"Yes, please. I've done several of hers in the past and they were really helpful in a lot of ways."

Hearing a throat clear behind her, she turned and saw Zeke standing there. "Angelina? Got a few minutes? Thought we could go over a few things before Tuesday," he asked.

"Uh, sure...um, Renda?"

"Go on, sweetie, I've got the girls," Renda said.

Standing, she followed Zeke into the clubhouse and to his office. She noticed once again how tall he was and admired his salt and pepper hair which was reminiscent of Sam Elliott's in the movie "Roadhouse". Shaking her head at her musings, she sat down and waited for him to speak.

"Okay, I won't take much of your time today, but wanted you to have a bit of a heads up regarding the mess you were taking over," he said.

"I know from Dex that your former accountant did some skimming. He told you I hold forensics computer certifications on my license, didn't he?"

He looked at her stunned. "No, he didn't mention that. What does it mean exactly?"

"I should, hopefully, be able to trace where and how he skimmed and then put checks and balances in place, so it won't happen again," she responded.

He nodded, even though what she said still sounded like Greek to him. "Okay, well, we have several businesses owned by Heaven's Sinners MC. We've got a twenty-room motel, a pizza parlor, a beauty shop, a daycare, and a bar and grill," he told her.

"So, five businesses in all?"

"Well, actually six. We've got the garage as well. For some reason, nothing has been making money for a few months and that's what led us to finding out that he was stealing from us. I don't hold out any hopes that we'll see what he stole, but I'd like to get my Brothers back on track with regards to what they were earning."

She looked over the stack of files that he had handed her, one for each business. At first glance, it looked like they used one master checking account, which was a no-no when it came to allocating the funds properly. Glancing back at him, she said, "Okay, I know I'm going furniture shopping tomorrow, but it won't take all day, so I may start going over some of this tomorrow if that's okay?"

He looked at her in stunned disbelief. "Are you sure? Tuesday is soon enough."

"Well, it looks like you have one master checking account that you were paying all of the businesses' bills out of and that won't do. You need a separate account for each business with an account for the MC that monies from each can be transferred into to pay the Brothers. It's how I set it up in South Georgia and it has checks and balances to keep what happened to you from happening. Each of the five businesses there are all earning a profit and while I've not looked closely, the size of the town here appears to be about the same as there, so it would stand to reason you should be as well."

He sat back, again stunned by the words coming out of her mouth. He had suspected that the accountant was lying when he said one account would work for all the businesses since they were run by the MC, but what she said made more sense. The items for the garage were large ticket usually, and it should have been pulling in a lot of money even with the initial outlays they sometimes made against parts. "Okay, if you want to do that, feel free to do so. I'm still clearing Tuesday so we can go over this together and come up with a plan, okay?"

"Okay. Do you think before we jump into the paperwork you could take me around to the businesses so I could meet the managers? I think while we're trying to get this all straightened out that some of the reins need to be pulled back some."

"In what way?"

"I think that until I can make heads or tails out of what has happened and see if I can find the missing monies so that they can hopefully be returned, all invoices, bills and payables should be handled by me. Once we get new accounts set up for each business, we can set up vendor accounts with each vendor that the business uses with a capped limit that must be approved by whoever you appoint. By meeting with the managers alongside you, hopefully you can make them understand that this is most likely temporary until we get everything fixed and back on track."

At that, he smiled. She didn't realize it, but she was already aligning herself with his chapter and the word *loyalty* flitted through his mind.

Man, he was handsome but when he smiled? Off the charts gorgeous she thought before mentally shaking her head at her musings. She was there for a new start and that didn't include looking for an old man. She had had one of those and needed to be content with her lot in life.

"Okay, let's do that then. I'll come by and pick you up around eight o'clock Tuesday morning, you can drop your girls off at the daycare, and then we'll grab some breakfast before I take you on the grand tour," he said.

"Um...how much does daycare run?"

"Angelina, you'll get a discount because you work for the MC and you're a part of the family. Plus, I know that most days, you'll keep your girls with you, correct?" he asked her.

"Yes, unless that's a problem?"

"Not a problem for me so long as the work gets done," he told her.

"That shouldn't be an issue at all, but I'm glad to have use of the daycare initially because I suspect I'll need uninterrupted time while I dig."

"Then we have a plan. Now, c'mon, let's return to the rest of the group and relax, okay?"

"Okay. Thanks again, Zeke. For everything."

He looked down at her and said, "My pleasure, Angelina."

Chapter Six

Waking up the next morning, Angelina looked at the clock and realized she was up early enough to have some quiet time. It was rare because the girls kept her busy, but she tried to squeeze in a daily devotional whenever possible. She no longer felt any guilt because she didn't spend hours in prayer or reading. God knew the hand she had been dealt and He had to realize she was doing the best that she could.

An hour later, with her bladder telling her that her time was up, she closed her bible and got up to face the day. Going through her morning routine, she dressed comfortably knowing that with Renda, shopping was often a marathon event and comfort was key. As she made her bed and straightened things up, she heard the giggles of her daughters and smiled. *Laser, I wish you could see them* she thought for the gazillionth time.

***

"Are you sure this is the store?" she asked Renda for the fifth time. "It seems a little much just for me, don't you think?"

Eva spoke up from the backseat where she was playing with the girls, saying, "Yes, this is the store. No, it isn't too much. Now c'mon, I have some ideas and want to see if we're on the same page or if I completely misread you!"

Walking through the store just holding her purse felt strange, however with Renda taking one and Eva the other, she decided to enjoy just being. A sales clerk headed in their direction, smiling when she saw Eva. "Eva! How are you? How's Preacher? What can we help you with today?"

Eva took a few seconds to answer her questions before finally saying, "June, this is Angelina Jones, she's MC family and has just relocated here from our South Georgia chapter. We need living and family room furniture."

June looked over at Angelina as if to size her up before asking, "Are these two cuties yours? I ask because that will help determine the fabric for clean-ups."

"They are mine but I'm a bit old school and they aren't allowed to wander the house with food or drink."

"Ah, a wise mom, that's for sure," June responded. "Come this way, do you have any idea what you want?"

Angelina looked at Renda and said, "I didn't even think to get the room measurements! Dang it all. Uh, June, I don't want it to look overcrowded. I'd love either a chaise at the end of a couch or a recliner at the end of a couch. The girls and I enjoy cuddling and watching movies on the weekends."

Eva spoke up before June could and said, "June, it's the house over off Main Street, I think the flooring department took care of that so you might have the room dimensions on file."

"I know which house it is and yes, we do. Give me a minute to go hunt them down while you browse, okay?" she asked as she headed toward the office.

As she looked around, she tried to visualize what *she* wanted. While the furniture she and Laser had was okay, it had belonged to him and was typical male-dark, heavy, leather-and she wanted light and airy to fit the feel she got from the house. Coming around a corner, her breath caught as she saw what she had been thinking of in her mind's eye. A couch with a chaise on the one end covered in a durable fabric that would hold up against two little girls' climbing, a loveseat with coordinating pillows, and what she always called a "big momma" recliner-one that was wide enough to fit her and two little girls. "Renda? Eva? What do you think of this one for the family room?" she asked.

Both women came up alongside her and looked at the set. "I like it," Renda finally declared. "It suits you and your personality, sweetie."

"I like it as well and think it will fit in the family room with room to spare," Eva said.

"Okay, ladies…ah, I see you found our cottage dream set! I was going to recommend it based on the room size because it will fit nicely while still allowing some floor space for your two cuties to play!" June said, having come back with the room dimensions.

"Then it's settled. I'll take this one. What about lamps? I'm not crazy about the ones used," Angelina asked.

"They come with the set but can be swapped for ones of your choice. Let's go look over here to see what you'd prefer," June told the women, leading them through to another section where lamps were prominently displayed. A lively discussion once again ensued until they finally agreed on two table lamps and a floor lamp that would go behind the recliner.

Another room, more furniture chosen for the "formal" living room, and they were done with a delivery date and time set up for later in the week. Eva took out her phone and texted Preacher, saying, "I'll let him know so he can have a few Brothers available to move things around."

"Thank you, Eva. I know the delivery guys usually do that but it makes it easier to have it done all at once," Angelina said. "Now, I had a list of things I needed to get, can you get us to the local department store before we have to feed the girls? I figure we've got maybe two hours before their behavior starts to deteriorate."

***

Later that afternoon, shopping done, Dex and Renda headed back to South Georgia, and the girls down for their nap, Angelina went into her new home office. She picked up the first folder and soon found herself immersed in numbers as she worked to create spreadsheets and a viable plan that would help them get back on track. Three folders in, she found the first discrepancy and made a note of it and then started to trail it back, deciding to find where the monies had gone.

When she heard the girls stirring, she backed up her computer and marked the folder she was working on because once they went down for the evening, she was going to see if she could go further.

"Hi my babies! Let's go potty and then go outside and play for a bit before dinner, okay?" she asked her daughters.

As they giggled through their bathroom routine, she thought about how fortunate she had been with them both. Even though she had been alone during the pregnancy save for Dex and Renda and some of the other old ladies she had been close to, it had been a relatively easy one and both girls were easygoing and well-behaved for their age. Grabbing them snacks and juices along with a bottle of water, she herded them out the back door where they immediately took off toward their new playhouse. Shaking her head, she pulled a chair down and got out her phone so she could snap pictures of them as they played.

An hour later, she called a halt to their playtime, eliciting a few complaints but not many because they were hungry. Getting them washed up and into their chairs, she dished up the spaghetti she had made earlier in the day and sat down to eat. Hearing the doorbell, she put her fork down and said, "Be good, girls and stay at the table while Momma goes to see who is at the door, okay?" Receiving nods, she headed to the front door and was surprised to see Zeke standing on the porch.

Opening the door, she looked up saying, "Hey, Zeke. Is everything okay?"

"Uh yeah, was in the neighborhood and thought I'd stop in to see how you made out today while shopping."

"Well come in, I've got the girls at the table eating spaghetti."

"I didn't mean to interrupt dinner…" he started to say.

"You didn't…that is, we just sat down. Would you like some? There's plenty."

Kind wafted across his soul. "That would be great if it's not too much trouble."

"No trouble at all," she said as she held the door wider. "What would you like to drink?"

"Whatever you have is fine."

"Beer, water, soda?"

"Water works for me. Too late in the day for more caffeine and I don't like to drink when I'm on my bike."

Dang, she had been in her own little world if she hadn't heard a bike she thought. Back in the kitchen, she dished up a plate of spaghetti for him and got him silverware and a bottle of water before sitting back down. The girls, thrilled with an audience, were both jabbering away and she watched as he smiled and nodded at them even though a lot of what they said was gibberish.

"Preacher said you found what you were looking for this morning. Any problems?"

"No, none. Eva knew the salesclerk and she was very helpful in the whole process. Since I'm not big on shopping, it worked well for me!" she told him.

"You don't like shopping?"

"Eh, not so much. I don't mind shopping online but going with two toddlers makes it challenging at times and they get tired and cranky being cooped up in a stroller or in a cart. I'll probably shop more with them once they're older, and use the times when I take them to daycare to grab things I need for the house," she replied.

Over dinner, he told her a little more about what their chapter was involved in and was surprised when she volunteered to help with the local orphanage. "Why?" he finally asked.

"Why not? There aren't enough good families to take kids in but every child deserves to have someone in their corner, loving them and teaching them and cheering them on. If I can do that in some capacity, well, then it makes it all worthwhile. Has...has anyone ever thought about becoming foster parents to these children? They do so much better in an actual home versus a group home."

He stopped and looked at her. Here she was, a single mother with two toddlers and she was worried about *other* children? Before he could say anything in response, she continued, saying,

"Because if not, maybe we can approach the administration to find out how to make that happen."

"I like that idea and will bring it to Church to see if other Brothers and their families might be on board before we approach them. I think you're right and even our single Brothers could possibly assist with the older kids."

"They're usually the ones harder to place. I should know," she said.

That's right, she had come out of the foster care system he thought. He suspected based on what little he did know that her memories weren't all that great, but he wasn't going to press the issue. Looking at the clock, he realized he needed to head out to pick Thad up from practice and said as much.

"Do you want to take some for him?" she asked, already up and looking for a plastic container. "I can never make just a little bit and there's more than enough even for a starving teenage boy."

He laughed at her description of Thad-he was all that and more and seemed to have a hollow leg. "Seeing as he's running cross country and they've got a meet tomorrow, that would be perfect. He tries to eat more carbs the day or two before a race for energy."

"Then it's settled," she said handing him a plastic container filled with enough spaghetti to feed his boy. "I hope he does well. Do we need to postpone tomorrow so you can watch him run?"

"No, we don't need to postpone it-he doesn't run until six tomorrow evening so we will have time to work and I'll still be able to make it," he told her.

"Okay, just checking. I know I'd want to be there so forgive me if I presumed incorrectly," she softly said.

He reached out and tucked an errant strand behind her ear, not knowing why he did so, before he said, "I try to never miss a meet. In fact, most of the Brothers come out and cheer him on which is kind of funny seeing as most of the other parents are in khakis and polo shirts, and the Brothers are in their jeans, T-shirts and cuts."

She started giggling and then outright laughing as the visual came. "Oh I can only imagine!"

"It's not too bad here in town because folks know us and Who and what we represent, but the out of town meets? Yeah, that's a little more challenging and we usually take our cuts off before we get there so we don't scare off the general population."

"That's a shame that people are so judgmental."

"It can't be helped, Angelina. It's just how most folks are hard-wired."

She looked up at him and he saw the sadness lurking deep in her eyes. "I wish it wasn't like that though. It can play hell on a person's sense of self-worth."

"Yes it can," he replied as he opened the front door. "I'll see you tomorrow morning, yeah? Make sure you lock up."

"Thanks for stopping by, Zeke. See you in the morning."

Chapter Seven

As he waited for Thad to come out of the locker room, he mentally replayed the conversations he had already had with Angelina. The words *kindness, grace,* and *loyalty* came to mind once again as he thought about the things she had said and how she had interacted with his Brothers and their families. He huffed out a breath as he shook his head over his musings. It had been a long time since he had felt any interest in a woman. He hadn't been celibate but also hadn't wanted a relationship with anyone-choosing to take care of his needs as impersonally as possible. Meeting her, however, had stirred up feelings he had thought were long buried. He still didn't know why he hadn't just called her earlier. No, like some love-struck kid, he had gone over to her house. Yet, despite his interruption on her evening, not only had she let him in but she had fed him! The truck door opening had him looking at his son who was climbing in and tossing his duffel bag into the back seat.

"Hey, Dad. Thanks for getting me, Toby couldn't stay late," Thad said.

"No problem, Son. Never has been and never will be."

"So…what's for dinner? I'm starved. Coach wants us to make sure we carb up."

"I've got some of the best spaghetti I've ever had in a container in the back for you," he replied as he navigated out of the parking lot.

"Your spaghetti isn't that good, Dad, and you know it," his son said, already reaching in the back for the container. "Uh, Dad? Why are there two carseats in the back?"

He chuckled a little before saying, "Angelina has two little girls and I'll be taking her around tomorrow to the businesses to meet the managers."

Thad perked up-he had never heard *that tone* in his dad's voice before and knew it had something to do with the woman he had heard relocated up to the North Georgia chapter. While he didn't remember his mom at all and was grateful to the old ladies and his grams for all they had done for him growing up, he had missed having a mom. Someone who would listen to him and give him advice about girls and hold him accountable. "So is she the one who made the spaghetti?" he finally asked.

"Yeah, I stopped by to make sure she didn't have any problems today while furniture shopping and she asked me to stay. She's a nice woman."

Thad thought about what his dad had just said. He couldn't remember a time when his dad mentioned a female. Like ever. Sure, he talked about and to the old ladies, but they were family. Well, this one was too, he guessed, but it was different. "Hate I missed yesterday, Dad, but Coach wanted that extra practice for tomorrow," he said.

"You missed some good brownies that she brought. But Eva said she planned to bring them every week so you won't miss them again, I'm sure."

"You didn't bring me any?" he asked, the sound muffled by his mouthful of spaghetti.

"Don't talk with your mouth full. No, I didn't. You snooze, you lose."

"Dang, Dad, that's kind of harsh, don't you think?"

"Nope. Now, you got any homework you need to finish up? With the meet tomorrow, you may as well go ahead so you don't get behind."

"Got some reading to do and I figured I would get that done once I shower. Practice was intense today and Andy got hurt, so we all need to be ready to up our runs," he finally said, having polished off the container. "Damn, Dad, that was some good spaghetti!"

Zeke glanced over at his son and saw him licking his lips. He could give him shit about cursing, but why bother? Instead, he simply said, "Use your words, Son. Use your words. And remember, some girls don't like guys who curse every other sentence."

He caught himself as he nearly rolled his eyes-his dad *hated* when he did that-and simply said, "That was not used as a curse word, Dad, but as an exclamation of appreciation!"

Zeke started chuckling-his boy had a point because *damn* it had been some good spaghetti!

✱✱✱

With Thad off showering before he did his homework, Zeke grabbed a beer and headed out to his back deck. Taking a long pull, he thought again to what Dex had told him before he left. *"Listen man, Laser was my best friend and I know he loved her in his own way, but she deserves more than what he gave her. Will you do me a favor and keep an eye out? She's young and attractive and I just don't want anyone to take advantage of that fact. It's not my story to tell, but she had it rough before we came along, and I've watched her grow into a confident young woman. Renda and I want the best for her and have been praying that someone would see what we see."*

He thought about Gayla. They had been young when they hooked up and when she found herself pregnant, he had done the right thing and married her. But a few years into it, she had decided she wanted "more" and had left him and Thad to make her own way in the world. He hadn't gotten a divorce, convinced that no mother would stay away from her child, but she had ended up dying. Looking back objectively, he could see that they likely wouldn't have lasted, she was needy, sometimes manipulative, and very self-centered, all qualities that he didn't like in anyone much less a woman. His thoughts then drifted to the woman he had met the day before and he inwardly smiled. She had to be scared shitless, coming to a new town and into a new chapter knowing no one and yet she had a smile for everyone she met and was already displaying loyalty to the MC.

A noise behind him had him turning to see Thad, fresh from his shower, coming through the door with a fresh beer and a bottle of water, his book tucked under his arm. He smiled, thanking God for the goodness that was his son. They weren't "buddies" but he enjoyed being around his old man just chilling and he knew that when he was no longer in "dad" mode, their relationship would expand further. Settling into the chair beside him, Thad handed him the beer and opened his book. "Dad?"

"Yeah, Son."

"Sorry for giving you shit earlier about the carseats. If I met someone who cooked that well, I'd put carseats in my vehicle too."

He shook his head at his son's statement. "She's taking over the books and while she has an SUV, it's a smaller one and I'd be cramped so this is easier. I'm picking her up in the morning and introducing her to the managers so she can unravel what Jay did and get us back on track." The MC wasn't hurting, not by a longshot, but it still galled him that they had trusted Jay to look after their best interests and he had burned them like he did. He was glad they weren't a club that took retribution on themselves, choosing to let God handle it.

"Looking forward to meeting her, especially if she cooks like this!"

They settled into a companionable silence, the only noise the occasional flipping of a page as Thad read for his assignment. Zeke enjoyed the quiet but he had something on his mind and wanted to feel his son out before he did anything about it.

"Thad?"

"Yeah, Dad?"

"I know I haven't dated much. How would you feel if I started dating?"

Thad stopped reading and looked at his dad-*really* looked at him. He saw a man who was confident in his own skin, who knew how to lead others while not being overbearing. He knew his dad probably got lonely and after thinking about it for a few minutes, he finally said, "Dad, my mother has been gone a long time and you've never really dated since then to my knowledge. There's no way I can expect you to remain single for the rest of your life because honestly? I don't think that's what God has planned for you."

Out of the mouths of babes he thought as he stared at his son. "I just don't want to do anything that will hurt you, Thad," he responded. "I know it wasn't easy growing up without a mom around."

"No, it wasn't, but that wasn't your fault, Dad. *She* made a choice to leave us," he said, matter-of-factly. "And honestly? From what I've heard, you two probably wouldn't have lasted."

Deciding it was time to go back to safer topics, Zeke simply said, "We will never know the answer to that one, Son. Suffice it to say, I am thinking about dating again and just wanted you to know. Now, what say we go raid the fridge and see what else you can carb out on?"

Chapter Eight

With the girls bathed and down for the night, she headed into her office to get the few boxes unpacked. Once the books were up on the shelves, she arranged the pictures and knick-knacks around, knowing that some would move into the living and family rooms after the furniture arrived. *At least the boxes are emptied* she thought as she broke them down and carried them out to the garage. She made a mental note to ask Zeke if there was someplace they could be stored in case another Brother or family had need for them.

***

Back in the house and changed for bed, she decided to look over what she had found again which led to more searching. Hours later, eyes burning from staring at the computer screen, she sat back satisfied. Not only had she found where and how the monies were siphoned, but she knew where they were sitting. She looked at the clock and saw it was going on ten so she sent a quick text to Zeke instead of calling him in case he was in bed already.

Angelina: Zeke? It's Angelina. I've found the money.

Zeke: Really?

Angelina: Yes. I've printed everything out so that we can go over it in the morning.

Zeke: Sounds good. Now, go get some rest, please.

Angelina. I will, just wanted you to know. Good night.

Zeke: Good night, Angelina.

***

He thought about her text as he prepared for bed. She was definitely more than he had expected and he decided he would let Dex know in the morning how glad he was that she had relocated. As he drifted off to sleep, he felt peace deep within.

Chapter Nine

When her alarm went off, she realized quickly that it was going to be "one of those days" and felt as if she was behind the power curve trying to get through her shower, get dressed and get the girls up and going. Hearing the doorbell, she rushed to grab the door and barely glanced at Zeke standing there. "Hey, good morning, I'm running a bit behind. I'm sorry. Come in, we should only be a few more minutes."

Sensing her distress, he followed her into the kitchen where he could see that for whatever reason, the girls weren't being cooperative with their breakfast. He sat down next to Melora and started talking to her. "Hey pretty girl, are you giving your Momma a hard time this morning?"

Melora looked at him wide-eyed before she grabbed a handful of oatmeal and flung it to the floor. He held in his laughter because he could see how upset Angelina was getting and went to get some paper towels to clean up the mess. "Cherub? If they're not hungry now, trust me, they'll eat when lunch is served at the daycare. They may not be that hungry right now."

She looked at him. He didn't look upset or strained or any other kind of distress that she was feeling. Instead, he was calmly cleaning up the messes the girls had made and once that was done, he went and got first one and then the other and took them to the sink to wash their face and hands. The girls weren't always like this first thing in the morning, but every once in a blue moon they got finicky. Never had she been more grateful for an extra set of hands than this morning. "Thank you," she finally said as she worked to clean up the rest of their breakfast mess. "I think you're right about them eating at lunchtime. I swear more landed on the floor than in their mouths."

He glanced at her as he put the girls down and said, "I commend you for doing this on your own. I had a hard enough time with one and you do it with two."

She smiled at him, saying, "Most mornings go a bit smoother than today, that's for sure. I think it's all the changes in a few days that has them off a bit. I hope they won't be a problem at daycare."

"They'll be fine. Marta runs it and has a way with kids. She'll have them playing and laughing and giggling in no time."

"Oh! I met her yesterday. It'll take me a bit to put the faces with their names, but I'll get there. Just one of my quirks I think and when I meet a lot of folks at once, like yesterday, names escape me completely."

"You'll get them, don't worry."

Gathering her purse and the files and the girls' bag, she looked at him and said, "I think we're ready. Again, I'm sorry we're running late."

"Don't worry about it, Cherub. We've got all day, remember?"

Cherub? What? Why was he calling her that she wondered? Deciding against asking right now, she walked out the front door with the girls and when he was also out, locked the house up and headed toward her SUV.

"Uh, Angelina, thought we could take my truck."

"Oh! I'll just get…"

"No need, I got carseats already so we're all set," he told her, taking Cailyn's hand.

She looked at him in total astonishment. "You got *carseats* for your truck?"

"Yup," he replied, working to get the little girl into the carseat as she came around to the passenger side and put Melora in.

"But...but why?" she finally asked.

"Because your SUV is kind of small for my height and I know that we will be working together to straighten things out and will need to go to the businesses at times. This way, you don't have to worry about swapping your seats in and out," he told her. By now, he was at the passenger door waiting to help her in, something she appreciated since it was up off the ground and she knew her gracefulness wouldn't extend to getting into his truck without help.

"I wouldn't have minded swapping them out, Zeke," she said softly. "There wasn't a need for you to go to that trouble or expense."

"Cherub, it wasn't any trouble. By the way, Thad was very appreciative of the spaghetti last night."

"Oh! I'm so glad. He wasn't there Sunday, was he?"

"No, his Coach called an extra practice for today's race. Seems one of their guys is injured so he wanted to get in some conditioning work and a run in preparation."

"That's good-like I said, I get faces down pretty easy and will match them to the names, but I was worried I had met him and forgotten already!"

✱✱✱

As they headed toward the daycare, he glanced at her and saw a profile that he could get used to looking at every day. *God, where did that come from?* He pointed out things he thought might interest her and showed her where the park was at, thinking it would be a good place to take the girls.

They talked about inconsequential things, he told her how long he had been a part of Heaven's Sinners and when he had taken over as President. She told him how challenging it had been going to school with two newborns and how grateful she was for the old ladies, especially Renda and her closest friend, Debbie, whose old man, Pongo, was the South Georgia chapter's secretary.

"I've got to ask-how did he get that as his road name?"

She started to giggle and then burst into laughter. He didn't think he'd heard anything so musical sounding in his life and was transfixed for a few moments. Finally composed, she said, "His youngest child *loved* watching '101 Dalmatians' and he got to where he could quote whole sections of the movie. One day, when he used a quote in Church, Dex looked at him and told him that from now on, his name was Pongo and it stuck!"

He laughed, more at her telling of the story than anything before he said, "A lot of the guys don't have road names. It's not something we necessarily require, but occasionally, one sticks and we give it out, y'know?"

She nodded. Several of the guys in South Georgia didn't have road names, but there were plenty who did so she was used to how they rolled.

They reached the daycare and he pulled in and as if it was the most natural thing in the world, he came around and helped her down and then went and got Melora out. She tried not to be disloyal to Laser's memory, but there were so many things he didn't do for her and opening her doors was one of them. Walking in behind him, she saw the woman she had met the day before and smiled.

"Hi, Marta! I'm so glad you're here. The girls will remember you and that should make it easier for them to stay," she said.

"They'll be fine, Angelina, I promise. And I have your number in case we run across anything we need help on, but I've been doing this all my life now. Is there anything I need to know?"

"I've started potty training them and the daytime accidents are minimal. I've found that if I take them before and after they eat, the success rate is greater. Also, I do use a pull-up during naptime but am about to stop that soon."

"Well, it sounds like they're on target. We have the lead instructor in their room and she'll work on some basics like colors and shapes, nothing too strenuous but we try to get them ready for the four-year old Pre-K room. There are four helpers in there because that is the age when so many are potty training, so they should be good there as well. Any food issues? Particular dislikes?"

She thought for a few moments before saying, "They'll eat just about anything and have no known allergies that I'm aware of right now. They kind of goofed off at breakfast so I think they'll be hungry by lunch!"

"Looks like we're all set. I'll call if we have any issues. Do you want to see their room?" Marta asked.

"Yes, please. C'mon, sweet girls. Let's go see your new class!" she said.

Once again, Zeke held Melora's hand as they walked to the three-year old classroom. Seeing the bright colors and the toys that were arranged by interest, she knew the girls would have a good time. As she leaned down, she hugged and kissed them both before saying, "Momma will see you two in a few hours okay? Listen to your teachers and remember your manners."

"Yes, Momma."

"Okay, Momma."

Leaving them was hard and Zeke could see her take a deep breath before she smiled brightly and looked at him, saying, "You ready to go?"

He nodded at her and put his hand on the small of her back to guide her back out the door, never expecting to feel the zing of *something* shoot up his arm. He saw her shiver slightly and wondered if she had felt it as well, but didn't ask. Once again, he helped her into the truck and she smiled gratefully, saying, "It's a downside being this short. Thanks for the lift up, Zeke."

He smiled up at her and replied, "Anytime, Cherub. Anytime."

What was with the 'Cherub' comment she wondered. As he got in, she cleared her throat before asking, "Zeke? Several times now, you've called me 'Cherub' and I was wondering why?"

Well damn he thought. *She wasn't afraid to ask the tough questions after all.* "Does it bother you?" he asked her.

"No…not really. I mean, Dex calls me Angel, Laser called me Lina, most of my friends either call me by my full name or variations, so I answer to a lot of things," she finally told him. "But you still didn't answer my question. Why?"

"Because you're petite. Because despite your petite size, you have a fierce protectiveness that surrounds you with regards to your girls. Because you have an angelic face."

Hmmm, interesting she thought. "Okay."

"Angelina, it's my nickname for you. If you aren't comfortable with it, I won't use it, okay?"

"Zeke, it's fine. I just...I just didn't know why is all."

✳✳✳

At the diner, he asked for a back booth so they would be away from folks, and when the waitress came over asking for their drink orders, he watched as she asked for water. He knew she wasn't a coffee drinker, but from watching her he knew she liked her caffeine cold and asked the waitress for a Diet Coke for her and a coffee and orange juice for himself.

"Cherub? You order what you want, yeah?"

"Okay."

Looking over the menu, she saw they had several things she liked so she finally asked him, "What is good here?"

"Everything."

"Can you narrow that down? I don't think I can eat French toast, scrambled eggs, bacon, and hash browns!"

"Why not? Eat what you can if that's what you want," he told her.

As the waitress came back with their drinks, they went ahead and placed their orders and she went with the "giganormous" plate as she called it, much to his delight.

He watched her reach into the tote she had carried in and took the folder she proffered. "Here are the notes I made on each of the businesses. I also have the notes on where the monies are at so you can give it to whoever you need to and hopefully recover it all."

She waited for him to look everything over before she continued. "Like I told you on Sunday, you definitely need separate business accounts for each business, and a main MC account to put the Brothers' portions in so that you can see the money trails better. Also, it'll be less of a headache at tax time to have them separated like this instead of lumped together. And, at a glance, I think the reason your old accountant could do what he did is because you carry such a high balance in the MC account. He could take a little here and a little there and it wouldn't be missed. I didn't see where anyone else but him was involved, which is a good thing to my way of thinking."

He continued looking through the pages she had printed off and grabbed a pen out of his pocket and started jotting notes alongside. He agreed with setting up separate business accounts and finally said, "When we're finished here, before we start the business tour we're going over to the bank to get the accounts set up, okay?"

"I think that's a good idea. I had another one that I forgot to write down."

"What's that?"

"You've got so much in the MC account, I would suggest setting up a few money market accounts that can be rolled over. They'll earn interest and aren't high risk, but it will keep you from having too much in the account at one time. If you want to take it to Church and figure out what a good balance would be, those won't be hard to get set up."

Damn he thought. She definitely understood this life and was looking out for the MC and hadn't been here a week yet. "I like that idea. Any others?"

"I think the vendors need to be condensed some, except maybe the garage because I know you have to get parts and they aren't always cheap. We can ask the managers who they use now and I can do some research to see who will give you the best bang for your buck."

"Okay, I agree with you there as well. If you think you have time to do it, please feel free to do so."

"Also, and this is definitely something we'll need to talk about with the salon manager. I know from the women in South Georgia that there are different seminars offered that will give them the continuing education they need. I think that the business should cover those trips, maybe the cost of getting in and their hotel?"

"I'll have to take that one to Church but off the cuff, I don't see an issue with it. I know they need it to keep their licenses, but since they *are* working for an MC business, we should cover it or maybe half of it."

The waitress interrupted them, bringing a tray with their food on it. "Need anything else? Jellies? Ketchup?"

Angelina looked at the table and at Zeke, who shook his head no. "No, thank you, I think we're good."

"Okay then, holler if you need anything, yeah?"

Zeke, taking a chance and wondering what on earth he was doing, reached across the table for her hand. "I'd like to pray over our meal if that's okay?"

Her heart warmed. Laser had been a believer, but he didn't pray over their meals and they didn't do any kind of couple's devotional. *Stop comparing them* she told herself. "I'd like that, Zeke," she said softly.

He prayed over their meal, holding her hand and when he was finished, gave it a gentle squeeze before he released it and began eating. Over breakfast, they continued to talk and he gently probed about her growing up years.

She closed her eyes, it had been years since she had talked about "before" but for some reason, she needed Zeke to understand her. *He already does* she heard in her soul, loud enough that she looked around thinking it was audible to everyone. "Well, let's see, my dad took off when my mom was pregnant with me. She did what she could to take care of me, but because she had no family support, she became homeless. That led to a drug and alcohol addiction and I was removed from her care when I was six. I was bounced around from house to house until I ended up with the Cook family. They were very religious and we were at their church every time the doors were open. They put up a good front out in public, but at home, it became a living hell. I never did anything right and they "knew" I was going to end up like my mom. I aged out at eighteen and had nowhere to go and ended up on the streets. With no job, I panhandled some but was, in essence, starving. The church wouldn't help me, the shelters were full of men who were scary, so I stayed in the shadows and did what I could to stay clean and fed."

He looked at her and saw that the pain from her past was at the front of her eyes. "I'm sorry, Cherub, I didn't mean to bring up bad memories for you."

Smiling at him, she replied, "It's okay. My life changed for the better the day that Dex and Laser found me. They had come into the store where I was angling to shoplift and Laser saw me slip a sandwich in my pocket. I had enough change for a drink and was hoping it would hold me over for a day or so. Laser came up to me and put his hand on my shoulder and scared the hell out of me. He told me that they would buy me dinner, I wouldn't look good in orange and he felt God had another plan for my life."

"How long before they took you in?"

"Well, Dex took me home that day to Renda, who took one look at me and adopted me, even though she's only about eight years older than I am. They gave me a room and got me clothes and made sure I ate. Most importantly though, they showed me the difference between religion and a relationship with God. I'll be eternally grateful for that day."

"I'm glad they found you, Cherub. God definitely has a plan for your life."

"I hope so. It's been a bit challenging these past few years. Without all the help from the folks at Heaven's Sinners, I wouldn't have been able to finish school and who knows what would have happened with the girls. So, I'm grateful despite being on my own."

He looked at her and said, "I know it's challenging being a single parent. If you need help, please don't hesitate to reach out, yeah?"

"Okay. Thank you."

Deciding to change the subject, he said, "So on Saturday night, we're having a party at the clubhouse for us grown-ups. Are you going to come out? We cater in the food and hang out and drink and dance."

"I'm not sure. I would need to find someone to sit with the girls."

"We can check with Eva. Her daughter, Tally, is always looking for babysitting jobs to fund her mall trips."

"Ah, a teenage girl who likes the mall? Should be a good fit then," she said, laughing.

"Are you ready? We'll head over to the salon first so you can talk with Eva about Saturday night before we get down to business."

"Sure. Did you want to go to the bank first though?"

"Yeah, we better do that so you have that information. And I need to stop by the attorney's office and give him what you found so he can see about getting our monies back."

"Okay. Yes, I'm ready. Thank you for breakfast."

"My pleasure, Cherub."

***

Leaving the bank after a lengthy hour-long visit, his head was swimming and he was again grateful that the woman at his side was there. She knew her stuff and made sure that the accounts were set up properly and that there were alerts in place to prevent what had happened before from happening again. He made sure she was on all the signature cards even though she said that wasn't necessary because sometimes, he wasn't available to sign checks. When he told her that, she agreed.

Now at the salon, they waited for Eva to finish with her client. He noticed that Angelina was jotting notes again and he leaned in and whispered, "What are you doing?"

"I'm jotting down the products they sell for retail so I can do a search on potential vendors. I know next to nothing about this industry at all so will definitely be relying on Eva to steer me in the right direction."

Eva came out with her client and smiled as she came toward Angelina. "Hey girl! Glad to see you today. Let's go to the back so we can talk, okay?"

"Sounds good. I love the look of the place, Eva! Very open and spacious, yet soothing at the same time."

"Thank you. Several of the old ladies are also stylists and we wanted a place that represented 'us' but also allowed the general public to feel comfortable as well."

"I think you managed to achieve that quite well if the books are any indication."

Once back in the little office, Eva pulled out a file and handed it to Angelina, saying, "Here is a list of the products we use and sell. Zeke had mentioned you might have some ideas?"

Angelina took the file and opened her own with her notes. "Ah yes, do you use a lot of different vendors? I was thinking that if you did, we could research and see if we could get a better deal using one vendor instead of several."

Eva glanced at Zeke and then said, "We usually order from wherever we get the best deal, but if we could find a vendor where we could get a good deal all the time, it would definitely save money. We found through trial and error that using quality products yielded better results."

"That makes sense to me. What about the retail end? Do you want me to search to see what kind of sets I can find? I know there's usually a decent mark-up on those. And regarding the color line you use, how do you keep up with the inventory? Do you find yourself running out and having to place an order unexpectedly?"

Eva sat back and thought. "Y'know, we have had to do that a few times and it ends up costing more in shipping and rush fees. Do you have any suggestions?"

"Well, keep in mind I *don't* know your industry, okay? What if we created a spreadsheet of the colors you *do* use, as well as any other chemicals like perms and such, and if you're able to, y'all can go through your client lists and see who is coming up on needing a service. We can stock for your existing clients and have a margin of safety for new folks who come in who aren't sure what they want. And I'm sure highlights are a constant, so getting good bleach and developer would be important, right?

"Girl, for not knowing our industry, you sure know a lot!"

"Thanks to my girl, Debbie. She owns the salon in South Georgia and I guess I picked up some stuff listening to her over the years. She's going to be up here soon so I definitely want to introduce you two!"

Zeke interrupted, saying, "I think they're coming up with Dex and Renda for the weekend and will be at the clubhouse on Saturday."

"I had no clue! Guess I'll definitely plan to be there Saturday night then. I know Dex and

Renda will likely stay with me again, what about Pongo and Debbie?"

"We've got rooms at the clubhouse, Cherub, so they can stay there. You don't need to feel as though you have to host everyone who comes up, y'know."

"I don't feel like I do, Zeke, but Dex and Renda? They're family. Not that Debbie and Pongo aren't, but they love the girls so I don't mind them coming."

Eva, meanwhile, looked back and forth between the two of them. *Cherub* she thought. *Hmm interesting. Wonder what Preacher will have to say about all of this?* She decided she was going to be talking to her old man to see if what she was thinking was far-fetched or within the realm of possibility because she had never seen Zeke act like he was around Angelina.

"Okay, Eva, I think we've gotten what we need. We've switched to a separate banking account for each of the businesses so for the time being, Angelina will be paying the vendor bills and invoices that come in for all of them until we get things turned around."

"What about payroll? I usually pay the girls on Friday for the week before. They, of course, deal with their cash customers, but the credit card customers pay the shop and I issue checks the following week once they've cleared the bank."

"If you can get me the information on Mondays, I'll reconcile the charges against the bank account and can have the checks written out and ready for Zeke to sign either Tuesday or Wednesday and then drop them off to you."

"That will work. Generally, the shop is closed on Mondays for inventory and deep cleaning, so maybe you and I can meet for lunch and I'll have all that together for you. We can tweak the inventory sheet. My goal is for the business to grow, obviously, so that we *all* make money while serving our community."

"Go ahead and get input from your stylists as well, they may have ideas we didn't discuss and I am open to whatever will help streamline this for you and make it easier on you so you can do what you enjoy best, not paperwork."

Eva looked at Zeke before saying, "I really like her, Zeke! You know how much I don't like paperwork and if her being here means it's down to a minimum? I'm good with it one hundred percent."

Zeke started laughing. He knew how much of a headache the paperwork gave Eva because Preacher shared it often, especially on the nights when she was bent over the books instead of paying him attention. Thinking about Saturday had him saying, "Eva? Do you know if Tally already has a babysitting gig on Saturday night? With Dex and Pongo coming up especially, I'm sure Angelina would like a night out with grown-ups."

Eva thought for a second before she replied. "I don't think she does but I'll call her once school is out to check and if she doesn't, I will bring her over this evening if that's okay Angelina? That way, you two can meet and she can meet the girls."

"Thank you, Eva. I would definitely like to meet her because Zeke mentioned y'all do the grown-up parties at least once a month and I know I'd like to have the adult interaction!"

"Then it's a plan. Is that all you two need from me? My next client is due any minute now and I need to get ready."

"I think so, yes. If there's anything else, I'll jot it down and let you know this evening, okay?"

"Sure thing, girl. I'll text you later when we are on our way, okay?"

"Okay, that works."

As she watched them leave, Zeke's hand on the small of Angelina's back, Eva sent up a quick prayer that whatever was happening was doing so according to His will. It was about time her old man's long-time friend found his forever and she had a feeling it was in the shape of a petite, strawberry-blonde woman named Angelina.

***

They went by the rest of the businesses with the same results and Angelina got a feel for the people she would be interacting with on a weekly basis. All of them were happy to have the bulk of the paperwork taken off their shoulders so they could focus on increasing profits and ensuring their customers and employees were happy. Since she liked numbers, she felt it was a win-win situation all the way around.

Looking at the clock and seeing it was close to lunch, he looked over at her and saw her staring out the window, lost in thought.

"Penny for your thoughts?"

"Oh! I was just running everything through my brain that I've learned today. I can see I have much to learn about several of your businesses and hope you don't grow tired of my questions until I get it all squared away in my brain. Numbers I know, but pizza dough? Not so much," she answered.

He laughed before saying, "Ask away anytime, Cherub. Except on Sundays. I don't want you working yourself to the ground. We work to live in this MC, we don't live to work, y'hear?"

She had heard that philosophy for years now and knew they believed it fully. While every working member of the South Georgia chapter worked hard, they played just as hard and it was nothing for them to organize week-long family runs to the beach or even up to the mountains. She was getting the impression that the North Georgia chapter was the same. "I know, Zeke. And I promise I won't work too hard, but initially, I know I'll be putting in a lot of time until stuff gets turned back around."

Pulling into a restaurant so they could eat lunch, he parked and then turned to her, saying, "Look at me, Cherub."

Ah, the President tone again she thought as she turned her head.

"I am serious. Take your evenings with your daughters. Meet some of our members. I know a lot of your friends are in South Georgia, but am hopeful that some of the old ladies here will become part of whatever you women call them these days-your girls? Posse? Whatever it is, you need to be able to relax."

"I understand, Zeke."

Over a late lunch, they went over everything and she took a few notes so she could make sure she had it all straight. "When do you want to get together to go over this again, Zeke?"

"How about Friday? That will give you a chance to go through everything you've gotten today and maybe formulate some action plans."

"Okay, I think that will work."

"And don't think you need to be tied to your desk from nine until five every day either. If you or the girls have appointments, take care of them, yeah? I know you'll get the work done and I know once we get it all streamlined, it will give you a lot of extra time. Work to live."

She started laughing. "Did I give you the impression I'm a workaholic or something? I promise, I'm not but I want to be able to get this turned around for y'all quickly so that the Brothers are compensated for what they lost and I am prepared to spend the little bit of extra time that will take to accomplish that fact. Most of the time once the girls go to bed I'm at loose ends anyhow, so I may dabble some in the evenings, at least until we get caught up."

He looked at her and saw the determined look on her face and realized she wasn't going to back down. "Fine. Just not all night long, okay?"

"Okay, I promise."

***

They finished up around three and went back to get the girls. Seeing how happy they both looked took a weight off her shoulders that she wasn't aware she was carrying.

"Hi my babies!" she said, crouching to allow them to come into her arms so she could hug and kiss them. "Did you have fun today?"

Jabbering commenced and she caught a few words, mostly from Melora, that let her continue talking to them both. "You colored? And learned what a circle was? You'll have to show Momma when we get home what things we have in the kitchen that are circles, okay? C'mon, now, Mr. Zeke has been driving Momma around all day and needs to get home so he can watch his son run a cross country meet."

Taking their hands, she walked over to their cubby and got their bag. Looking over at the instructor, she asked, "Would you prefer if I brought some labeled clothes for them to leave here? Or do you want me to bring a bag every day?"

"Whichever is easiest for you, ma'am. If you bring some labeled clothes, we'll have them in the event of any accidents, and we have a washer and dryer here so we can wash any soiled clothes and put them in the bag so you aren't faced with a smelly bag at the end of a long day."

Angelina laughed and said, "I would appreciate that a lot. Okay, I'll bring them some extra clothes tomorrow to leave here "just in case" and I will also bring their bag every day. Did they do okay today?"

"They were great. A little shy at first, but once they saw the other little ones playing, they jumped right in."

"I'm glad. Say goodbye girls," she said, prompting them to use their manners with their new teacher.

"Bye bye Miss Jenny," the girls sing-songed.

"Bye, Cailyn. Bye, Melora. You two be sweet for your Momma tonight, okay? I'll see you tomorrow."

"Yes, ma'am."

Zeke held out his hand and wasn't surprised when Melora put hers into his much-larger one. She looked up at him and said, "Hi, Mr. Zeke."

"Hello, pretty girl. I'm glad you had a good day today. Do you like your new playhouse?"

"Oh yes, we play and play. It's a lot of fun."

"I'm glad," he told her as they crossed to the truck and he helped get her into the carseat.

Driving Angelina and her girls back home had his mind thinking of things he wasn't sure he should be thinking, at least not so early. But there was *something* about her that drew him in and so he sent up another quick prayer that God would give him a sign.

Chapter Ten

Angelina pushed back from her desk and stretched with a sigh. It had been a long week but she had made some serious headway getting each of the businesses' books back on track. She had spent a lot of time online doing some vendor searches and finally found vendors willing to set up accounts the way she wanted that would best benefit each business. She had gone to lunch with Eva a few times, and she also met the rest of Eva's stylists. All of them were thrilled with the vendors she had found, and after more discussion with Zeke concerning the upcoming *Premiere in Orlando* hairshow, she had mentioned it to Eva. She knew from her friend, Debbie, that those hairshows helped stylists improve their skills, with classes that covered advanced techniques and skills. She chuckled remembering Eva's ear-splitting shriek of excitement followed by her proclamation that Angelina's hair was forever "on the house" for getting that perk for them.

Gathering the files she would need for the morning's meeting with Zeke, she backed up and shut down her computer, then went and got something to drink before she checked on the girls one last time. Now comfortable in yoga pants and an oversized T-shirt, she reclined in bed and read. She felt content for the first time in a long time and knew a lot of it had to do with the local President. He wasn't intrusive, but was always around and had made himself available to her frequently as she had come across areas of concern. She had spent the day before at the garage so she could understand how their inventory worked. It seemed that basic supplies like oil filters and oil and spark plugs, that sort of thing, were stocked rather haphazardly. After pouring over customer receipts, she saw that they could do better ordering in bulk and once she pointed that out, Zeke had one of the Brothers rearrange an area of the stockroom to hold the supplies she ordered. They came up with a way to alert her when another order had to be placed and she was thrilled to see that even the mechanics themselves were happy about making their lives easier.

As she drifted off to sleep, a word wafted over her soul, *kinsman-redeemer*, and it left her wondering what God might be trying to tell her.

***

She woke the next morning and could feel the beginnings of a migraine. Since she knew it would only get worse, she took the milder of the two medicines she had hoping it would stave off the worst of it until she could get done with her meeting. She took a quick shower and proceeded to get ready before going in and waking up the girls.

"Good morning, Mellie and Caycoo. How are my babies this morning?"

Watching them wake up was something she wouldn't tire of soon she thought. Melora tended to be "awake" as soon as her eyes opened while Cailyn was more like a little sloth, slowly moving around and usually not very communicative until she had been awake for an hour or two. This morning, however, they both got up easily. There was a field trip to a local petting zoo with baby animals and they were excited about seeing the animals.

Breakfast done, she got the girls cleaned up and was checking their bag when the doorbell rang. "Come in, it's open," she called out. As Zeke opened the door, she could see the frown on his face and quickly said, "I knew it was you from the sound of the truck. I didn't unlock the door until just a few minutes ago."

"Cherub, you still need to be safe and check the door, yeah? You're a woman living on her own and even though it's a safe town, things happen. Promise me you won't do that again, okay?"

When he put it like that, it made sense she thought. "Okay, Zeke. I promise."

"Good. Now, where are those two pretty girls? I have a surprise for you two today since you're going on a field trip!" he asked as he pretended not to see the two little girls standing there, giggling. "Ah, there you are! Do you want to go see what's in the truck?" he asked.

"Yeth Mr. Zeke!"

"Please Mr. Zeke!"

Taking both girls by a hand, he looked at Angelina and said, "I'll get them in and buckled while you lock up, yeah?"

She smiled softly before saying, "Thank you."

He walked out with both girls jabbering about their upcoming day and got them into the back seat, telling Cailyn to climb over to her seat as he buckled Melora into her carseat. Both girls finally buckled in, he grabbed the bag that was in the front seat and opened it up to give them both a pair of little girl sunglasses full of sparkles, both were heart-shaped but one was purple and the other was pink. He was helping them make sure they were on properly when Angelina got to the truck. "Oh look at the movie stars in the backseat!" she called out as she opened the passenger door.

"Hold on, Cherub, and I'll help you," Zeke said.

"Okay. Trust me, I need a ladder to make this climb," she replied.

He walked over to her and tucked an errant hair behind her ear before saying, "Ready?"

She nodded then felt his arms around her waist as he lifted her up into the truck. "Thank you, Zeke."

"You're welcome, my Cherub."

My Cherub? That was different she thought smiling to herself. *Please, God, let this headache hold off until I get home.*

As he got into the truck, he thought he caught a flinch from Angelina and he took another look at her. She looked like she was in pain so he asked, "Cherub? You okay this morning?"

"Ah yeah, I sometimes get migraines but haven't had one in months. I was caught by surprise this morning."

"Do you have anything you can take?"

"I have two different medicines, one causes me to sleep and the other doesn't. Since we were meeting this morning, I took the non-drowsy one."

"Has it helped at all?"

"A little bit. I'll take the other one when I get back home."

"We could have rescheduled this morning," he finally told her as he navigated to the daycare.

"I'll be fine, Zeke, promise."

***

The girls dropped off, they headed to the diner for their breakfast meeting. Once again, looking over the reports and notes she had made, he was impressed with her thoroughness. It appeared she had gotten vendors together for each business so that bulk orders could be placed that had free shipping or even in some cases, decent percentages taken off when a certain amount was ordered. He looked up at her and winced when he saw the pain in her eyes. She never said a word but he noticed she didn't eat much either.

"These look good, Cherub. How about I sign the checks and we'll drop them off quickly. Then you can go home and take the other medicine, yeah?"

She sighed before saying, "That might not be a bad idea. This one is shaping up to be rather ugly. I'm sorry."

"Then let's get this show on the road. The sooner we're finished, the sooner you can start feeling better."

***

Making their rounds, she was pleased that each manager liked the suggestions and advised that she would get their inventory sheets on Monday so that she could begin the process of placing orders for them.

As he headed back to her house, he got the sense that she didn't need to be left alone, so when he pulled in, he got out and helped her out. He walked in behind her and said, "Cherub, don't think you need to be left alone for some reason and I try to heed those nudges I get. You go get comfortable and take your medicine so you can lay down, yeah?"

By now, the pounding in her head had been joined with nausea and auras around her eyes. She merely nodded and then headed to her room. When she stumbled into the wall, she found steady hands helping her into her room and directing her to the edge of her bed. He took off her shoes and then asked, "Where are your comfortable clothes?"

"Hanging…a pair of yoga pants is hanging up behind the bathroom door," she finally stammered out.

He got her pants and then, when she wobbled some more, he quietly said, "Trust me, Cherub, yeah?" before he removed her jeans and helped get her yoga pants on. He tried not to think about how soft her skin was or how nicely she was packaged, but he was a man after all. Once she was changed, he got her into bed and then asked, "Cherub, where is your medicine?"

"Kitchen cabinet above the coffeemaker."

"I'll be right back." He went into the kitchen and found the medicine then grabbed a bottle of water. Back in her room, he had her take the pills and then, without thinking, smoothed back her hair and kissed her forehead. "Sleep, Cherub. I'll be here."

***

She woke up disoriented, an after-effect of the medicine. However, she was headache-free and that was worth the few seconds it took to reorient herself to the here and now. Glancing at her alarm clock, she saw it was after seven and panicked-the girls! Climbing out of bed, she redressed in her jeans and slipped on her shoes and then headed down the hall, stopping when she reached the end and heard the giggles coming from the family room.

As she passed through the living room, she saw a large foot hanging over the end and glancing at the couch, realized it was a teenaged boy. *Hmmm, must be Thad* she thought as she grabbed a blanket and covered him. He looked like his dad only younger and she realized he would be a heartthrob in a few years, if he wasn't already.

In the family room, she stopped in the doorway and stared. Zeke was sitting on the couch with both girls curled up on either side of him and they were watching "Frozen".

He heard a noise and glanced back, thinking Thad was there. Seeing Angelina, he unwound himself from the two little girls and walked over to her. "Hey, Cherub, how are you feeling?" he asked, taking her face in his hands and looking down into her eyes.

"What? Oh, much better, thank you. How...how did the girls get home?"

"I went and picked them up and then we went and got Thad after his practice. Picked up some dinner as well and put yours in the fridge. C'mon, let's get you fed, okay?"

"I...uh, thank you, Zeke. Now you know why I take those as a last resort. They really knock me out."

"It's okay, Cherub. I'm glad you're feeling better. Do you get them often?"

"Uh, usually once a month," she stammered.

He thought about her answer as he herded her into the kitchen. With the flush on her cheeks, he figured that they likely struck close to her monthly cycle and decided he wouldn't embarrass her further by probing any more. Helping her get settled, he went to the fridge and pulled out a plate of food and put it in the microwave. "I hope you like meatloaf and mashed potatoes and green beans," he finally said.

"Comfort food? Absolutely. Nothing better," she responded. "Did the girls…they haven't been any problem, have they?"

"Not at all. And they've managed to charm Thad. In fact, I think they wore him out."

"That's possible. Did they have fun today?"

He started laughing as he regaled her with the stories they told while coming home and was rewarded by the giggles she couldn't contain as she visualized their adventures. "Thank you, Zeke, for everything today."

"My pleasure, Cherub. Can I ask a question?"

"Uh, sure."

"What all have you done for your migraines?"

"Well, I had a neurologist down in south Georgia, but I guess I need to find another one up here. That's a heckuva commute just to go to a doctor's appointment," she stated.

"I reached out to Eva and she gave me a few names for you to call," he told her. "Also, she apparently gets them from time to time and utilizes a chiropractor and a massage therapist. Might be something worth you looking into, yeah?"

She looked at him with a shocked look on her face, not believing that this man would go to the trouble to do some research for her. "Uh, I don't know what to say. My doctor back home was more of a traditionalist and wouldn't listen when I would ask about different therapies to try. I don't mind taking the medicine but with the girls, it's hard so there have been times when I've had to power through."

Power through? Remembering the pain she was in earlier he said, "Cherub, I can't fathom how you managed to do that because I saw how much pain you were in earlier, remember?"

"You're a single parent, Zeke. You know how it works-sometimes we do what we have to do despite how we are physically feeling. I'm fortunate, however, that I had Renda when things got really bad, so I wasn't always alone."

"Well, I've written down the name of Eva's doctor for you. Make sure you call, yeah? I don't want to see you suffering if there's something that can be done to prevent it."

Kind wafted through her soul. Looking at him, she said, "Thank you. I'll call Monday."

"So you never said, is Tally watching the girls for you tomorrow night?"

"What…oh, yes. She'll be here around five or so, what time does it start?"

"If it's okay with you, I'll come pick you up around five thirty."

"I…I can drive, Zeke."

"I know you can, Cherub, but I want to take you."

"Oh."

He could see the confusion and doubt running across her face and decided to lay his cards on the table. "Cherub? I'm interested in *you* and thought this would be a good first-time date since we would be surrounded by Brothers and their old ladies."

"You...you are?"

"Yes I am. If you...you're not ready to see people, please let me know."

She thought about it for a few seconds and realized that while she would always miss Laser, there were so many things she liked about Zeke- she felt comfortable around him, he was easy to talk to and had an even-tempered demeanor, he didn't shy away from making tough decisions, and he was good with her girls. "No...the time for mourning is past, Zeke. I know Laser wouldn't have wanted me to grieve my life away and besides, I have two living, breathing reminders in the other room that he was a part of my life, right? I'd like to go with you as your date."

He silently exhaled, not realizing that he had been holding his breath, before saying, "Then it's settled."

Hearing silence from the family room, she looked at him before flying into the room, only to stop short. It seemed that Thad had woken up, stumbled into the family room and on the couch, only to fall asleep again. The girls had cuddled up to him and the three of them were sound asleep with the movie still playing. Zeke pulled his phone out and snapped a few pictures and then went over and gently extricated Melora from her spot on Thad, while Angelina picked Cailyn up. Tip-toeing out of the family room, they headed down the hall where he helped her get the girls ready for bed and tucked in.

Back in the kitchen, he saw she had barely eaten and asked, "Do you want me to heat it back up for you? You didn't eat very much."

"No, I'm okay. For whatever reason, that medicine makes me lose my appetite so I'm good with what I did manage to eat." With that, she took the plate and covered it and put it in the fridge. Turning, she saw he was right behind her and she stopped short.

"C'mere, Cherub," he said softly. She walked up to him and stood there, not knowing what he planned to do. Her heart was thinking *he's going to kiss me* and her mind was thinking *is it too soon?* He reached up with one hand and his fingers stroked her cheek as he looked down at her. "I want to kiss you, Cherub, but don't want to rush anything where you're concerned. Is it okay?"

Looking up at him, she nodded unable to say anything. He could see her pulse rate pick up and knew she was nervous and determined that he would go slow. Pulling her close, he threaded his fingers through her hair and leaned down to gently touch his lips to hers.

The *zing* she felt had her feeling as if she had come home and she sighed as she looped her arms around his shoulders and leaned closer, allowing him to take over. She didn't know how long he kissed her, she just knew she didn't want him to stop when he pulled back slightly and kissed the tip of her nose as he leaned his forehead against hers. "Been wanting to do that all week, Cherub."

"I…I'm glad you did, Zeke," she said, almost breathlessly, the emotions almost overwhelming.

"Gonna get my boy and head home now, Cherub, but before I do, can I have another?"

In response, she leaned up and captured his lips with hers. She ran the tip of her tongue across his lower lip, eliciting a groan from him before the kiss turned into something almost incendiary. As he pulled her closer, enveloping her in his strong arms, she could tell how she was affecting him which caused her to moan. A noise from somewhere behind them had her pulling away to see Thad standing in the doorway, rubbing his eyes as he tried not to gawk at the two of them. She buried her face in his chest as embarrassment at getting caught flooded her face in a becoming blush. He tipped her face up and leaned in close to whisper, "He needs to see adults showing affection, Cherub, and it's not as if we're standing here naked in your kitchen, yeah?"

Sparkling green eyes met his before she burst into giggles. "As if! I mean, not that I don't want…I mean, uh…well, hell," she stammered, unable to complete her thought.

"I understand, Cherub. But just to say, it's too soon, yeah? We'll know when it's right and believe me, we'll be sure that there are no interruptions by any children."

"Uh, dad? Did I interrupt something?" Thad asked.

"It's all good, Son. Just saying goodnight to Angelina."

"Yeah, I see that."

"Don't be a smartass, Thad. Especially not in front of a lady, y'hear?"

"Yeah, Dad. Sorry, Angelina."

She took pity on the teen and said, "It's okay, Thad. Oh! Wait until you see the pictures your dad took of you and the girls!"

"What? When?" he asked.

"A little while ago. You ended up in the family room sleeping on the couch and they curled up next to you and fell asleep as well. Did they wear you out this afternoon?"

"Naw, Coach ran us to death. They're really cute kids, Angelina."

"Thank you. And thanks for helping your dad with them while I was sleeping."

"He said you had a bad headache like what Aunt Eva gets and I've seen how sick she gets with those so I was glad to help."

Zeke watched how easily his son and Angelina talked and smiled inside. While he had dated very sporadically over the years, most of his relationships had been discreet because they were for one purpose only. He didn't bring them around Thad, but he had long ago decided that he would never get involved with someone who didn't accept his son. Seeing the two of them getting along? Priceless in his book and something else he filed away.

"You got anything you need to grab Thad? We need to head out. And before I forget, what are your plans tomorrow?"

"Nothing much Dad. I have some reading to do and an essay to work on, but it's not due until next Wednesday so I've got some time. What do you need me to do?"

"Well, Angelina's grass needs cutting, you mind taking care of it for her?"

Angelina started to protest but stopped when she saw the look on Zeke's face-for some reason, this was important to him so she was going to let him handle it as he saw fit.

"Yeah, I can do that, can I drive the truck over with the mower?"

"Nice try. No. I'll drop you and the mower off. Cherub, you need to do anything in the morning?"

"I already cleaned and did the laundry, so the only thing I have left on my list was the grocery store."

"Then how about I take you and the girls to do your shopping while Thad cuts the grass? We can be here around ten so it's not too warm out and likely back in time for lunch so he doesn't starve to death."

Angelina glanced at Thad and saw the slight grin on his face. "I think that will work and just so you know, Thad, if you *do* get hungry before we get back, feel free to help yourself, okay?"

Zeke rolled his eyes, which made her burst into laughter. "Cherub, you better double whatever you had on your list after that last statement! You have no clue how much a teenage boy can eat."

"This is true but I'm sure I'll figure it out. Like I said, he can help himself."

"Then it's settled. We'll see you ladies in the morning. Be sure you lock up," he told her, leaning in for a brief kiss.

"I always do," she replied softly.

Locking the door behind them, she waited until they had pulled out of the driveway before she shut the outside lights off, then went around and straightened things up and shut down the house. Heading into her room with a bottle of water, she couldn't stop smiling. *He had kissed her! And man, had she liked it. A lot.* She couldn't wait to see what the future held and went to sleep dreaming of him.

Chapter Eleven

Saturday morning dawned bright and clear and as Angelina got ready for the day, she found herself replaying the past week, especially last night. While she knew it wasn't fair to compare the two men, she thought about the way Zeke treated her *every time* he saw her. He held doors for her, helped her into the truck, wouldn't let her pay for any of their meals citing the fact that they were business meetings, and how even today, he had his son coming over to cut her grass while *he* took her grocery shopping! Laser hadn't been unkind, but he had never shown by his actions in his day-to-day treatment of her that she mattered. Then, of course, there was the way he kissed! *Holy smokes* she thought. That second kiss last night nearly had her forgetting that there were children in the house! Sighing happily, she realized that even though she had lived with Laser for six years, this was her first date.

Picking up her phone, she quickly texted Eva to find out what the dress code for the *adult* Saturday nights were because she didn't want to embarrass him. When Eva texted back to ask why, she took a deep breath before responding that she wanted to know because Zeke had asked to bring her as his date. Seconds later, her phone was ringing and Eva's name popped up.

"Oh my *God*, Angel, you have no idea what this means!"

"Well, good morning to you, too, my friend. Wait, what do you mean?"

"He has *never* brought a 'date' to a Saturday party. *Ever.* I knew it, I just knew it!"

"What did you 'just know' young lady?"

"I got the sense that first meeting the three of us had that he was interested in you."

"Oh really? I didn't find out until he told me last night."

"He *told* you?"

"Uh, yeah. Right before he kissed me."

Shit that woman had a set of lungs she thought as she pulled her phone away from her ear. "You calm yet?"

"Girl, you truly have no idea. I've been praying for him for a long time now, wanting him to find his forever. I think you may be the answer to those prayers."

"Just to say-it's our *first* date. Surrounded by family, remember?"

"Yeah, but again, you have *no idea* how massive that is!"

"Whatever. So, you going to clue me in on what to wear so I don't embarrass our chapter President?"

"Angel, we're not fancy. The old ladies usually wear jeans and heeled boots, a nice shirt, and our property cuts. Maybe a little more make-up, a little more hair fluffing, but honestly? Just be *you* because I think that's what he likes best."

"Okay, and he said it's catered?"

"Yeah. The guys usually drink beer, but I don't much care for it so we usually make frozen strawberry margaritas."

"Oh yum, my favorite!"

"Well, be prepared to drink and dance, my friend."

Hearing the girls, she told Eva she needed to run, then she went and got the girls up and into the bathroom to start their day, happy to have another accident-free night. Once in the kitchen, she looked at the clock and saw she had enough time to make pancakes and have them ready by the time Zeke and Thad arrived. If he was going to cut her grass, the least she could do was feed him. She set the girls up with some cartoons and juice, grateful that the doorway into the family room was wide enough that she could put their highchairs so they could see the television and not worry about the furniture.

Music on, bacon in the oven cooking, she had the batter made and the griddle heating when she heard the knock on the door. Because of his constant admonitions, she had not unlocked it before he arrived and was rewarded with a smile when she clicked the deadbolt and lock and opened the door. "Good morning, Cherub. Did you sleep well?"

"I did, thank you. How about you?"

"Took a little bit of time before I fell asleep, but I spent the time seeking some wisdom."

"I see," she said, not fully understanding what he meant.

He leaned in close and dropped a kiss near her ear and whispered, "Was thinking about you, Cherub, and that made it hard to fall asleep." He saw when realization dawned on her because her face turned a pretty shade of pink.

"Are you two hungry? I'm making pancakes and bacon for the girls."

Thad looked at his dad and then said, "I can eat."

"You were actually one of the reasons I started cooking."

"Me? Why?" Thad asked, confusion crossing his face.

"I figure that you'll need the energy since you're cutting the grass and it's *never* a good idea to go to the grocery store hungry," she replied, turning and heading back into the kitchen, where she poured the first batch of pancakes on her griddle before she checked the bacon.

"What can I do to help, Cherub?" Zeke asked as he went to the sink and washed his hands.

"Um, well, I have juice in the fridge, the girls are watching cartoons as you can see, so all that's left is to finish the bacon and make the pancakes."

"Let me get the syrup and butter out. Thad, can you set the table?"

"Sure, Dad. Where are the plates?"

"They're over the dishwasher and the silverware is in the drawer at the end of the counter," Angelina said.

Working together as if they had done it for years, within a few minutes, the first batch of pancakes was off the griddle and the bacon was cooling. Angelina took the two small plates and got them ready for the girls and before she had a chance to do it, Zeke and Thad had carried the highchairs back over to the table.

"Okay, Mellie and Caycoo, are you ready for some pancakes?" she asked them.

"Yes, Momma."

"Pancakes! Thank you, momma. Hi, Mr. Zeke," Melora said.

"Melora? Cailyn? Can you say good morning to Thad?"

Both girls looked at the teenager before they said good morning in soft voices. Zeke held in his laugh at how they pronounced Thad's name while Thad grinned at how cute the two of them were.

Before long, they were all seated at the table and Zeke blessed the meal, impressed at how even the girls bowed their little heads. Giggles abounded once they started to eat, and he realized it would probably be a little longer before they headed out to the store.

Angelina looked at him and said, "I'm sorry. I forgot how messy they get even with a little bit of syrup. I promise I can get them cleaned up pretty quickly."

"No worries, Cherub. I'll give you a hand and it'll go that much faster if you want."

"Thank you. At least my list isn't too long!"

"That wouldn't matter either, Cherub. Wouldn't have offered if I didn't want to do it, yeah?"

Since there wasn't much she could say to that, she merely smiled and nodded before she started clearing the kitchen table. She had found, through trial and error, that leaving the girls until last was the best plan of action. Zeke went to the sink and found a clean dishcloth and got it wet and wiped the worst of the syrupy mess off their faces and hands, while Thad rinsed dishes and stacked them in the dishwasher. She was amazed at how well they worked together and filed it away in her heart of hearts to look at later.

"Dad? If you two are good, I'm going to head out and get started, okay?"

"That's fine. Remember to stay hydrated out there. It's not too hot, but it'll take you some time to get it done and that will likely change if the weatherman can be believed."

"Oh, here, Thad, take one of these out," Angelina said, grabbing a cold Gatorade from the fridge.

"Hey, thanks! It's my favorite flavor, how did you know?" he asked as he opened the top and took a drink.

"I kind of took a guess."

"Good guess."

"Well, there's more in the fridge, as well as bottled waters. Please, help yourself, okay?"

"Thanks, Angelina. Appreciate it," Thad said as he walked out the back door.

"Are we ready to get these two monkeys into a bath?" Zeke asked.

She looked at the girls and saw that they had syrup on their pajamas too, so she went over and stripped them down to their pull-ups before she said, "Now we are."

He picked up Melora, who seemed to gravitate toward him for some reason, and headed down to their bathroom. Putting her down, he started the bath water and asked, "Do they get bubbles?"

"What's a bath without bubbles?" Angelina asked in return.

He poured some bubble bath in as she made short work of putting them on their respective potties. Business taken care of, she plopped them both in the tub and said, "Now, we're not playing this morning, my sweet girls, because we have shopping to do, okay?"

"Kay, Momma," Cailyn said, reaching for the sponge.

Meanwhile, Melora was fascinated with the bubbles and was completely oblivious to the fact that Zeke was bathing her, being sure to keep her hair dry since it had escaped the syrup.

Within minutes, they had both girls bathed and Zeke went to find them clothes while Angelina got them dried off. He came back in with matching sundresses and sandals and she bit back a smile. He may have raised a son, but he knew how to make her little girls beam, because he said, "I thought you two would like to dress up when we go shopping."

Giggles rang through the bathroom as they got the girls dressed and Angelina helped them brush their teeth before she combed their hair and put braids in, adding ribbons once she was done.

"Hmm, I'm going out with three beautiful ladies today," Zeke said, smiling at the picture in front of him. Leaning in, he kissed Angelina and whispered, "I can't wait until tonight, Cherub."

She smiled shyly at him before responding, "Neither can I. It'll be my first date."

Stunned. That was the word that crossed his mind-how had this beautiful woman never been out on a date. "Not even in high school?"

"Nope. Told you, the family I lived with was religious and they didn't believe in dancing and all that nonsense. Claimed it was all from the devil or some shit."

"Momma, you said a bad word," Cailyn said as she looked up at her mother.

"Sorry sweet girl. Momma will do better, okay? That's not a word for little girls to say, though, so don't say it."

Back in the bedroom, the girls grabbed their new "babies" and said "Can we go now in Mr. Zeke's truck?"

"Absolutely, as long as your Momma is ready," he responded.

"I'm ready, just need to grab my purse and phone," she said.

***

As they meandered through the grocery store and he watched her turn her nose up at the selection of fruits and vegetables, he remembered that there was a farmer's market on the square in town. "Cherub? Why don't you get what you need besides the fruits and vegetables and we'll run to the farmer's market."

"There's a farmer's market here?"

"Yeah, they have one every Saturday on the square, weather permitting."

She looked at her list and circled a few things and then said, "Okay, I think the other items I have should be okay while we're at the farmer's market."

"Brought my cooler, Cherub. Get what you need, yeah?"

"You…you brought a cooler?"

"Figured you would want to get stuff that needs to be kept frozen or cold," he replied.

"Popsicles! Momma said we were getting popsicles!"

"We can keep them cold, girls."

She smiled gratefully at him. As they got the rest of the items on her list, she felt something settle within. She almost felt like a family.

***

He stood and watched as she negotiated with the vendor and smiled with pride at how she had managed to get what she wanted at the price she was willing to pay and leave the man smiling. She had a knack for putting others at ease. He also enjoyed seeing her with her daughters. She was gentle but firm and he noticed, not for the first time, that they were very well-behaved without being robotic. Her love for them was evident in every word, glance and touch. As they meandered from booth to booth, he finally reached out and took her hand in his and saw her glance of surprise. The girls were riding in a wagon that they had available at the farmer's market and he was pulling it with his one hand, so he reasoned he had another hand that needed holding-hers.

As he intertwined their fingers, he gave hers a squeeze and once again felt that *zing* of something. He sent up a prayer asking for patience with whatever was happening, and got the sense that things might be happening a lot faster than he anticipated. Regardless, after a lot of quiet time and reflection, he knew he had to talk with Dex at some point this afternoon and let him know the lay of the land. Preacher had already reached out to him when he realized how much time they were spending together. He didn't care. At forty and with one bad marriage behind him, he felt that so long as he continued to seek His will over the situation, all would be well.

***

Finally finished, they loaded up his truck and got the girls buckled into their seats. He looked at the time and called the pizza parlor and placed an order for pick up, figuring that by the time they got back to her house, it would be time to eat again. "Cherub? Will you take my phone and send a text to Thad and let him know I'm bringing pizza and wings?"

"Sure, Zeke," she replied. Taking his phone, she sent Thad a text and was sure to let him know it was her sending it since his dad was driving, and heard the chime of an incoming text almost instantaneously. Looking at Zeke, she said, "He wants to know how many wings you ordered? Also, he said he's got the back yard mowed and trimmed, and has started on the front yard."

"Tell him I bought him his usual, and then got another thirty-piece bucket."

Thirty pieces? They must like their wings she thought as she texted back Zeke's response. When the phone chimed again, she looked at the response and burst into laughter.

"What's so funny, Cherub?" he asked as he glanced over at her.

"He sent back a bunch of emojis of dancing characters and what looks like a fist bump," she replied, still giggling.

He chuckled at her response and said, "He likes those."

"I do too, sometimes. They can definitely help convey emotion because sometimes, texts can be misunderstood," she replied.

He thought about what she said and finally nodded. "Yeah, I can see that happening."

"Do you know what time Dex, Renda, Pongo and Debbie are getting in?" she asked as he pulled into the pizza parlor.

"They should be getting to your place around the same time we get there," he told her as he put the vehicle in park, but kept it running. "Stay here, Cherub, so we don't have to wake the two sleeping beauties in the back."

She glanced over her shoulder and could see Melora sound asleep, her baby clutched against her chest. Turning around, she saw Cailyn in nearly the same position and then she smiled, seeing that they were holding hands. "Zeke, look," she said softly.

He stuck his head back into the truck and saw the two little girls sleeping, holding their babies with one hand and holding hands in the middle. Smiling, he took his phone and snapped a picture. "That's a keeper, Cherub. Be right back, yeah?"

She nodded and watched as he carefully closed the door and then walked into the pizza parlor. Her eyes grew huge when she saw him walk back out with four huge boxes of pizza and what looked like two paper grocery sacks holding what she presumed were the wings. He walked around to her side and she rolled down her window. He handed her the bags first, which she put on the floor, then he said, "Cherub, why don't you scoot over to the middle? The boxes are hot and I don't want you to get burned."

Thoughtful she mused as she unbuckled then slid over to the middle seat as he put the pizzas where she had been sitting. She buckled up and waited for him to get back into the truck. "Can you just make sure the boxes don't fall over?" he asked after he rolled up the passenger window.

"Sure," she replied, but as she reached her right arm over, he stopped her and cupping her face, drew her toward him so he could kiss her. Each kiss they shared ramped up how she was feeling about him and this one was no different. He possessed her mouth, leaving no doubt what his eventual intentions were where she was concerned and she was hard-pressed to disagree with where things were leading, even though it was fast. He finally pulled back but not before he feathered kisses across her lips, nose and forehead.

She couldn't breathe quite right and noticed that he was in the same shape, which caused her to smile inside. Running his thumb down her cheek and across her lips, he gave her a look that she couldn't quite decipher before he buckled up and proceeded to back out and head back to her house.

***

"Angel! You look great," Renda said as she came up to the truck, Debbie right beside her. Zeke helped her out on the driver's side and she found herself engulfed in the arms of her two best friends.

"Oh I've missed you, Debbie! Wait until you meet Eva, she runs the salon up here. You two have so much in common and I can't wait to introduce you," she finally said as she untangled herself to get the girls.

"We've got them Cherub, and Thad grabbed the food so you ladies might want to head inside before he devours most the wings," Zeke told the trio.

She smiled as she linked arms with the two women and they headed into the house. The guys carried the girls into their room and she woke each up enough to go to the bathroom before she laid them back down for their nap. They could eat when they got up. Closing the door, she headed to the kitchen where she found herself picked up and swung around by Pongo. "Pongo! You goof! Put me down before you hurt yourself," she told him.

The big, burly biker just laughed as he hugged her, saying, "Half-pint, you don't weigh much more than those babies in there."

"Whatever. Put me down so I can introduce you, yeah?"

"Not before you pay the toll."

She sighed before she threw her arms around his neck and loudly kissed each cheek. "There, you happy?"

"Well, I guess so," he said, mock disappointment on his face.

"Zeke, this crazy man is Pongo and that's his old lady, Debbie. Pongo, Debbie, this is Zeke, the North Georgia President."

Handshakes and that strange male hug thing that the Brothers did ensued while Thad stood there, bouncing from leg to leg.

Looking over at him, Angelina started to laugh. It was obvious he was hungry, but he was trying to be polite as the introductions were made. Deciding to take pity on the teen, she said, "Thad, can you grab the paper plates and napkins? They're in the pantry on the back shelf."

"Yes, ma'am," he said.

As everyone settled at the table, she went to the fridge and asked, "Who wants what to drink?"

"Do you have any tea, Angel?" Dex asked.

"Yes, as a matter of fact I do and you should be glad I love you because you know I don't drink it but for you and Renda, I'll make it all day long!"

"Angelina? Can I have some tea too, please?" Thad asked.

"Sure, honey. Who else wants tea?"

"Now wait, I thought it was for *me*," Dex said.

"Ha, no, I *made* it because I knew you two were going to be here, but there's more than enough for everyone. I've got lemonade and water and soda as well. Debbie? Pongo? Zeke?"

"Lemonade for me, girl," Pongo replied.

"I'll take a diet soda if you have any," Debbie said.

She gave her friend an incredulous look. "Does the sun rise in the east and set in the west? Of course, I have diet soda!"

"Cherub, do you have any coke?" Zeke finally asked after everyone else had gotten their drinks.

"Yeah, Zeke, I do," she responded.

Once everyone had their drinks and plates were made, Zeke blessed the meal and they ate. Talk over lunch was constant, with Dex and Pongo and Zeke talking about the different businesses and the women talking about the party that night.

"So are you settling in okay, Angel?" Debbie finally asked.

"Definitely. They're learning that I'm good with faces and the names take time and everyone has been beyond patient as I learn the ins and outs of their businesses. Once we're done eating, I want to show you the house, too, so you can see what the Brothers and old ladies did for the girls and I," she responded.

Zeke looked over at the woman who had pretty much captured him, even though she didn't have a clue, and said, "She's being modest. Not only does she have all the books in order, but she found the monies that the old accountant stole. The prosecutor is working to get it back and I know once he does, the Brothers are going to be thrilled."

Angelina blushed at his praise. She hadn't done it for that, she truly liked working with numbers and the challenges she had faced initially had been like a puzzle. She was glad she had solved it for them because they were family, even if she didn't know them all yet.

With lunch finally done, Thad excused himself and went back out armed with more Gatorade and water to finish the front yard. Angelina gave Debbie and Renda the tour, even though Renda had been involved in the furniture buying.

"Oh, Angel, I love your room!" Debbie said as she looked around. "It's so spacious and fits your personality perfectly!"

"Even though I spend a good part of the day in my office, I love being in here or in the family room," she replied. "Sometimes, I'll bring my laptop over to my sitting area and pull up Netflix and play on Facebook while I'm binge watching my shows. C'mon, I want to show you the playhouse the Brothers got for the girls."

As they headed out to the backyard, they passed the guys still sitting at the table and Zeke grabbed her hand to stop her. She looked down at him sitting there and saw a look on his face she couldn't decipher. He tugged some more until she was closer and then cupped her face before he kissed her.

In front of his brothers she thought before she gave herself over to his kiss. It was brief but she felt like it sent a message, although she still wasn't clear about what that was exactly.

In the backyard, the other two women looked at her with big eyes. "What?" she said.

"Angel, do you know what he just did by kissing you in front of Dex?" Renda asked.

"Not...not really. Care to fill me in?"

"Sweetie, he all but claimed you."

"Claimed me? Why? I mean, well, hell, I don't know what I mean," she stammered.

"Dex said that Zeke called him earlier today and told him they needed to talk. He said the words kinsman-redeemer, sweetie. Do you remember what we talked about a while back?"

Angelina thought for a moment before she turned and looked at her friend with wide eyes. "You mean…no, surely not. I mean, we haven't known each other very long. Hell, tonight is our first date!"

Debbie finally spoke up, saying, "Babe, that man has it bad for you. He watches you constantly and the look on his face? It's swoon-worthy."

Swoon-worthy? What the ever-loving fuck? Shaking her head, she looked at both of her friends before sternly saying, "Look, I've only been here what, two weeks? We spend a lot of time together but that's just because we need to get the businesses back on track."

Renda and Debbie looked at each other before they burst into laughter. "You keep telling yourself that, sweetie," Renda finally said. "Now, let's see this playhouse."

Walking into the playhouse, she smiled. The Brothers and old ladies had really outdone themselves. It looked like a miniature house with a living room, a kitchen and a bedroom that had been set up as a nursery for the girls' babies. In the little living room there was a small television that worked, which still had Angelina shaking her head. They had also run electricity and heat to it, and there was a window air conditioning unit. She knew that it was a playhouse that would grow with the girls.

Debbie looked around in astonishment. "This is fantastic! It's almost like a tiny house, isn't it?"

"Y'know, you're right! The guys did a great job and the girls spend a lot of time out here in the afternoons. Zeke said while my job isn't nine to five, when I pick the girls up from daycare, he wants me to focus on them, not the work. So, we usually come out here for an hour or two before dinner. In fact, I have a feeling their babysitter will be out here with them most of the evening, at least until it starts getting dark."

"How do they like daycare?" Renda asked.

"Oh my goodness! They're doing so well. They are nearly potty-trained for naps and overnight now. They've been learning their shapes and colors and even Cailyn is coming out of her shell more," Angelina replied.

"This move was a good thing in more ways than one," Renda said softly.

"Yeah, I think you're right. But I want to ask you two while you're both here-you don't think it's odd that all of this is happening between Zeke and I? I mean, whatever *this* is?"

They both looked at her, knowing what she had come out of and, to an extent, the life she lived with Laser and of course, what she went through after his death. Finally, Debbie said, "Babe, I gotta say this and please, don't take it the wrong way, okay?"

"Um...okay."

"We loved Laser, he was a good and solid Brother. But in a lot of ways, his fucked-up past kept him from giving himself to you fully. He loved you to the best of his ability, but babe? You deserve so much more and that man in there? I feel it down to my gut that he can give it all to you. And since I love you to pieces, gotta say, it's something I've been praying about for you for years now."

Angelina looked at Renda and was stunned to see her nodding her head in agreement. "He wasn't that bad, y'all. He got me off the streets, remember?"

"Yeah, babe, he did. But there were things he did that weren't right while you two were together and honestly? It's time you faced those cold hard facts. He could be a bastard even to those he loved and we know, especially with you living in the clubhouse, that you bore the brunt of that."

Angelina looked at her friends with tears in her eyes. She hadn't wanted to think about that part of her life with Laser or how cruel he could sometimes be. She knew he didn't really mean it, but his words and actions had hurt her countless times. She sank onto the little loveseat in the playhouse and covered her face as the sobs started and the tears came harder. She cried for the man he could have been. She cried for what their relationship wasn't. She was still sobbing when strong arms lifted her and carried her out of the playhouse and into the house and to her room. As the door closed and she was carried over to her sitting area, a part of her brain realized that it was *Zeke* holding her close.

"Shhh, Cherub, I've got you," he whispered as he stroked her back soothingly. "Let it go, sweetheart. Let it go and let God heal you fully from the past."

She cried until all that was left were hiccups. Unwilling to look at the man whose shirt was now soaked with her tears, she softly said, "I'm sorry."

"Why are you sorry, Angelina? There's no shame in tears and I think you've needed to get those out for a long time. Tears don't mean you're weak and to me, you are one of the strongest people I've ever met."

Hearing his words and the tone he said them in had her tilting her face up to him. He wiped her tears away with his thumb before he leaned down and softly said, "God has you here for a reason, my Cherub, and we're going to follow His will in all this, yeah?"

"Yeah, Zeke. I…I'm sorry I broke down like that. I…I tried to forget and push that all back and just remember the good stuff."

"Things buried have a way of coming back, my Cherub. I hate that you had that hurt in your life and I don't need to know any of the details unless you choose to share them with me, just know that I'm here and I'll listen and I'll never judge, okay?"

"Okay, Zeke. I should probably get cleaned up, I know I'm a hot mess."

"Most beautiful hot mess I've ever seen," he whispered. "Let's make some new memories, Cherub," he said before he claimed her lips in one of the sweetest kisses she had ever experienced before he picked her up and carried her into her bathroom and sat her on her vanity counter. He hunted down a washcloth and got it wet and then oh-so-gently wiped the evidence of her tears away. His touch was soothing and she found herself relaxing.

"C'mon, Cherub, let's see if those two little ones are ready to eat some lunch."

He helped her down and hugged her and she drew even more strength from the calm that radiated from him. Looking up, she traced his jaw with her hand and said, "Zeke, I have no clue what's going on here and I sometimes feel like I fell down the rabbit hole, but I have felt from the moment I arrived that this is where I'm meant to be."

Leaning down, he kissed her forehead before he said, "I feel the same way, Cherub."

Hand in hand, they went down the hall to the girls' room only to find it empty. Once back in the kitchen, they found the girls eating and entertaining the four adults sitting at the table. As Angelina looked at her family, she found herself blushing. "I...I wanted to apologize for breaking down on y'all," she started to say, only to be interrupted by Dex.

"Angel, no apologies are needed. Renda and I knew there was something not right for a long time, but there was no way to pursue it. We prayed constantly for His will to be done because we could see you slowly fading."

Pongo looked at her and the anguish on his face just about gutted her. "Half-pint, we owe you an apology. We knew and while we all talked to him multiple times, we couldn't get through. I want you to know this, though, every one of the Brothers that knew what was going on threw their protection on you. If he had laid a hand on you, and unfortunately, we knew it was coming, we would have demanded his patch and he would have been kicked out. You, however, will *always* be a part of the Heaven's Sinners family.

Always, Angelina, and you need to let that fact seep into your soul, y'hear?"

Since this was the most she had ever heard Pongo say, she couldn't do anything but nod. "Thank you for what you were able to do, yeah? It wasn't all bad, I had my girls and I had school."

"And now you're here and you're actually *living* not existing," Debbie said.

She thought about all they had said, then she realized that she was ensconced on Zeke's lap and neither Dex nor Pongo were looking all crazy-eyed, and it dawned on her that for whatever reason, God had brought her through all of that to be able to appreciate all she finally had. "This may sound crazy, but you guys have to know that He was walking right beside me through it all. He knew what was happening and while I don't ever understand the *whys* of why we have to go through valleys, I know it has made me appreciate the beautiful mountain I've found myself living on now."

"Momma?" Cailyn asked.

"Yes, sweetpea?"

"Playhouse now?"

"Use your manners."

"Please can we play in the playhouse, Momma?" she finally asked.

"Yes, my sweet girls. Let's go get cleaned up and go potty then you can go outside and play. And...Momma has a surprise for you."

"A 'prise, Momma?" Melora asked.

"Yes, my Mellie-belly girl. A surprise."

With minimal fanfare, they got the girls cleaned up and headed out to the playhouse. She saw that the guys had brought several of the deck chairs down in the shade and was grateful because with her fair skin, she didn't tan, she burned. Turning, she went to the freezer and pulled out three popsicles, then went out the front door and found Thad still cutting grass. She motioned for him to stop and said, "Here's your 'prise, Thad."

He looked at her in shock and said, "What?"

"Well, I got these as a surprise for the girls. I really try to limit their sweets, but it's getting hot now and they were so good this morning at the grocery store and the farmer's market. You've been great getting this taken care of for me. I'm sure you had something else you could have been doing with your friends or even your girlfriend."

"I...I don't have one of those. There's a girl and I want to ask her out but I'm not sure how," he confessed.

"Well, do you talk to her at all?"

"Yeah, we have a few classes together and she's on the cross-country team."

"Okay, any dances coming up?"

"There's the spring fling formal coming up in three weeks."

"Hmm, okay, well, why don't you ask her out for dinner and a movie and then if it goes well, ask her to that dance."

"You make it sound so easy!"

"Honey, nothing worth having is really easy, but if you two already have some things in common, then you have half the battle taken care of, right? Do you ever text or talk to her on the phone?"

"Yeah and sometimes we message on Facebook."

"Okay, so listen, Tally is keeping the girls tonight and I trust you won't do anything you shouldn't. Why don't you call and invite her over to hang out with you guys? I've got the movie channels and popcorn and stuff. And if her parents are worried, I'll see if maybe a prospect or someone can come over as well."

"You...you'd do that? For me?"

"Yeah, sweetheart. You're a good kid. Just let me know, okay?"

"Thanks, Angelina. I appreciate it, I'm going to call her now," he said, finally taking the popsicle.

She turned away and went to go back up on the porch and saw Zeke standing there, a sheen in his eyes. "Zeke? Are you...are you okay?" she asked.

"Never been better, Cherub. Never been better," he said, pulling her in for a hug. "Thank you for what you just did for him."

"I...I know I'm not his mother, but if...if what I think is happening with us is happening, he's going to be around and well, I know what it's like not to be included and to feel left out and I won't ever let him think he's not as important just because I didn't give birth to him. I'm probably closer to being an older sister if you want the truth, but that's okay. Just please, let me know if I ever overstep because that's not my intention."

He kissed her gently. He didn't think he'd ever get tired of kissing her and thanked God once again that she came into his life. "I will, Cherub, but I don't think you'll have to worry about that. Now come on, we're going to watch the girls play and *you* are going to go and lay down for a bit."

"I am?"

"Yes, you need to be rested for our date. We've got some dancing to do, Cherub."

She smiled up at him and took his hand as they went into the house. Seeing her girls, she laughed as she said, "I've apparently been sent to my room. I guess I'll see you guys at the clubhouse. Thank you for taking care of the girls, yeah?"

"Anytime, babe," Debbie said.

"Sweetie, go rest. We've got drinking and dancing to do tonight and we're gonna show these 'Yankees' how us South Georgia girls do it!" Renda said, laughing.

"All right, I'm going," Angelina finally said.

Zeke walked her to her room and closing the door, he pulled her into his arms. "Cherub, you feel so right here in my arms. I'm not questioning this any longer."

"Um, okay…" she said slowly.

Leaning down, he kissed her. All thought fled from her mind as he molded her to his body and she felt the strength that flowed from him to her. She knew he wanted her and she knew that she could push the issue, but instinctively realized that it wasn't what she needed to do right now. So, she let him possess her mouth. Even in the passionate embrace, she still felt cherished. And it was a feeling that she prayed she would have for as long as she drew breath.

Finally breaking the embrace, he softly said, "Go on now, Cherub, and lay down, yeah? I'll see you at five thirty."

"Mmm…okay, Zeke."

He left her standing in her room, dazed from his kisses with desire flowing through her body. She had never felt like *this* before she thought as she slipped her shoes off and grabbed a throw before she climbed onto her bed. Just before she fell asleep, she set her alarm so she would have plenty of time to get ready. Tally was going to be there at five and *Zeke* was going to be there at five thirty. She shivered in anticipation as she drifted off to sleep.

***

"You're going to be her kinsman-redeemer, aren't you?" Dex asked as Zeke came out on the deck. The women were down by the playhouse watching the girls and Thad had joined in and the two little girls, after finding out he had gotten a 'prise too, had declared he was their driver and the postman. From the look of things, he was having a good day, even though his companions were a bunch of adults and two three-year old twins.

Zeke looked at his fellow President and weighed what he wanted to say carefully. "I know the story, Brother, and I guess, in a sense that I will be that for her. But you've got to know that wasn't ever my intention, yeah? There's just something about her and while I have no clue where God is taking all of this, I'm praying constantly because that woman in there deserves only the best. I know I don't know it all and I've told her she can tell me or not, it won't matter, but from the way she broke down, I'm guessing things weren't all sunshine and roses with Laser."

"No, Brother, they weren't," Pongo said. "She put on a brave front around everyone, but we all have ears and we heard how he berated her behind closed doors. Even though he was a believer, I don't think he ever let Him fully heal him of his past. It was ugly and left nasty scars and unfortunately, even though he loved her in his own way, she took it all."

"I'm kind of surprised it took her so long to finally break down," Dex said. "We've been waiting for it for a long time, but it's like she blocked it all out and focused on the good, what little there was. And even though it's not our story to tell, Brother, you need to know what you're dealing with, okay? He cheated on her. Repeatedly. Sometimes, right in front of her at club parties. I know we don't have the club girls like a lot of clubs, but Brothers bring dates in and they bring their friends and he often availed himself of those friends. Not out in the open, of course, you know that we don't allow that shit, but she knew. And that woman sleeping inside? Never complained. Not once. She kept on loving him despite his actions. And I'm telling you now, Brother, his actions hurt her, but that *is* her story to tell."

Zeke merely nodded. He had a lot to think about and pray over. Giving man hugs, he let them know he'd be back to pick her up at five thirty and headed home. Well, technically the clubhouse. Thad had a room right next to his and while it wasn't ideal, it had worked for a long time. Only now, it wasn't working any more.

***

She woke up refreshed from her nap, the crying jag feeling like a distant memory. Thinking about the whole episode, she realized that in many ways she no longer had that heavy feeling that she had carried for more years than she knew. And, it dawned on her that Zeke had been right, the tears were cleansing and with them, she had released things she hadn't realized she had been carrying around. As that thought crossed her mind, another came wafting in-*You were not responsible for his actions, my Daughter*-and she realized that He had spoken to the very core of her soul.

Getting up and going to her closet, she searched to find the shirt she was thinking of and when she found it she pulled it out and looked at it critically. Not trusting herself to something so important, at least to her, she went in search of Renda and Debbie. Seeing her come out on the back deck, they left their spots by the playhouse and came up to see what was going on.

"Can you two keep an eye on the girls for a bit?" Angelina asked Dex and Pongo.

"Sure, Angel, you girls go get all gussied up," Dex said.

She rolled her eyes at him as she went back in the house. Following her back to her bedroom, Renda and Debbie stopped short when they saw the chaos. She had pulled out at least a dozen shirts and they were tossed on the bed. "I need help," Angelina told her two friends. "This is my first-ever date and I want to look nice."

Their hearts broke hearing that but neither let what they were feeling show on their faces. She needed them and that's what a girl posse did- they helped one another.

Going over to the pile, Renda looked at each shirt and finally pulled one out that was a deep raspberry color with flowing sleeves that ended a little below the elbow. It was light and airy, with a flouncy bottom. "I like this one best, sweetie. It will bring out your pretty green eyes. And I like the brown boots better."

"I agree. Now jump in the shower and get cleaned up so I can fix your hair," Debbie said.

"Okay, okay! I forgot how bossy you two were," Angelina said, teasing her two friends.

"Yeah, whatever. We miss you too, you know!"

***

Angelina looked at herself in the mirror with a critical eye; the outfit was perfect, her make-up done lightly and what Debbie had done with her hair was nothing short of masterful. Long, fat curls bounced along her back, and she had pulled a few pieces back in what she called a faux French braid, saying it helped make her eyes pop. She spritzed on a little bit of her favorite cologne and took a deep breath. *I can do this* she thought. I already know him; we get along well and have a lot in common. This is just taking all of *that* to the next level. As she was headed down the hall to find the rest of them, the doorbell rang and she changed directions to answer it.

"Hi, Tally, come on in," she said to the teenager. "I'm so glad you were able to babysit for me and I promise, I won't give you such short notice next time, okay?"

"It's not a problem, Miss Angelina. My mom said that Thad and maybe Amelia might be here tonight too?"

"Ah yeah, about that. You'll be the one in charge of the girls, but apparently, Thad likes Amelia and I thought it would be a good first non-date before he asks her to y'alls spring fling formal."

"Oh! She's one of my closest friends and has been hoping he would ask her!"

"Well, you didn't hear it from me. I think one of the prospects is going to be here as well to offer her parents some comfort that a bunch of teens aren't here by themselves."

"That's fine. You look really pretty tonight."

"Thanks, sweetie. I had my two besties here to help me out. C'mon, I think Dex and Pongo need rescuing and that will give me a chance to help you get the girls inside so they can eat."

"Okay, lead me to them!"

Out in the backyard, she looked at the playhouse and sure enough, the two little girls were still playing. "Melora! Cailyn! Time to come in now, girls," she called out.

"Okay, Momma!" they said, almost simultaneously.

They came running up the back steps, jabbering a mile a minute and stopped when they saw Tally. "Girls, do you remember Tally? She came with Miss Eva the other night and she's going to be watching you two tonight while Momma goes out. Thad and Amelia are coming over as well, but Tally is the one in charge of you two, do you understand?"

Wide-eyed, they both nodded at her. "Can we watch a movie, Momma?" Melora asked.

"I'm sure you can, but not until after you have eaten dinner and taken your baths. You've both been playing hard outside today and need one, okay?"

"Okay, Momma," Cailyn said.

"Now, come on you two and let's at least get your hands and faces washed before you eat."

"Tally? There are plenty of leftovers, but if you want me to, I can place an order for pizza because I'm pretty sure we demolished the ones we had at lunch."

"I'm sure whatever you have left is fine, Miss Angelina. Now, c'mon girls, let's go and get clean!" she said as she led the two little girls down the hallway to their bathroom.

Feeling a little bereft, she went into the house and stopped short. Standing there just watching her was Zeke. "Hey," she said softly.

He walked closer never taking his eyes off her until he was standing directly in front of her. Running his thumb in a caress down the side of her face, he leaned down and kissed her lips before saying, "Hey yourself, Cherub. You look beautiful."

"Thank you. Did…did Thad come with you?"

"No, I have the prospect taking him over to get Amelia. Thank you for doing this for him. He has been walking on air all afternoon."

She giggled at the image before saying, "I'm happy to do so. Oh, and apparently Tally and Amelia are good friends and she said that Amelia has been hoping that Thad would ask her to that dance, so I think it's a pretty sure thing."

He shook his head as he smiled down at her. "I think he plans to tonight. We'll see, right?"

"Yes, we will. Uh, what is that?" she asked as she looked at the kitchen table where a gorgeous bouquet of flowers sat.

"For you, Cherub. Wasn't sure what your favorite flower was so I had a mixed bouquet created."

"They…they're beautiful, Zeke. Thank you!" she said, turning to give him a quick hug.

I could get used to her in my arms he thought as he placed a quick kiss on her forehead. "You ready to go?"

"Yes, let me just give the girls a kiss goodnight and tell Tally we're leaving, okay?"

"Okay, Cherub. I'll wait for you right here," he said.

She went into the girls' room and saw that they were busy showing Tally their things, including their beloved Cabbage Patch dolls. "Girls? Momma is going to be going now. Come give me kisses, okay?"

They ran over to where she was crouched and she wrapped her arms around them, hugging them tightly as she kissed them and said, "Now, you remember to behave for Tally, okay? Mind your manners and when she tells you it's bedtime, you need to go and not argue. I love you my babies, so much, and I'll see you in the morning, okay?"

"Love you, Momma," Cailyn said softly.

"I love you, Momma," Melora said. "You look pretty Momma."

"Thank you, Mellie."

"Tally? If you have any questions or problems, don't feel bad about calling or texting me, okay?"

"I'm sure we'll be fine, Miss Angelina."

***

"You ready?" she asked Zeke as she came back down the hall.

"Yeah, Cherub. You got everything?"

"Just want to grab my phone. I told Tally she could call or text if she had any problems."

He waited as she got the phone then led her out to his truck, where he helped her up. When he came around to the driver's side and got in, he looked at her and said, "Really liked it when you sat next to me earlier, Cherub."

She smiled at him as she slid over into the middle. "Is this better?"

"Absolutely," he told her. "Because I can do this," he whispered as he leaned in and kissed her. He then sat back and grinned at the bemused look on her face.

On the way to the clubhouse, he told her about the family run they would be doing that summer-they were going up to Maggie Valley in Cherokee. "We all go, Cherub. The businesses shut down for the week and our customers are used to us doing this from time to time as we give plenty of notice. You might get a little bit busier before we go, but you'll have a week of no spreadsheets, so it will be a good trade-off."

"That sounds like fun. The kids go too?"

"Everyone, Cherub. We have a few vehicles that go to haul the kids, but most of the Brothers and old ladies ride."

"Okay, well, I can drive one of the vehicles since I have the girls," she said.

Not if he had anything to say about it he thought. "I'll keep that in mind."

Arriving at the clubhouse, she was surprised to see how many people were around. "Everyone tries to make these, Cherub. You ready to go in?"

"Yeah."

He helped her out of the truck then captured her hand in his and walked toward the doors. Walking through, he fielded man-hugs and backslaps from his Brothers as he headed toward the table where Preacher, Dex, Pongo and their old ladies were sitting. "Hey y'all," Eva said. "Did Tally get there on time?"

"She did and when we left, the girls were busy showing her every little thing they owned," Angelina said, laughing.

"What's on the menu tonight, Brother?" Dex asked.

"Thinking it's barbeque but don't quote me. Preacher put the order in," Zeke said as he sat down next to Angelina.

"Which means that *Eva* put the order in," Eva said, laughing. "And yes, we're having barbeque tonight."

"Woman, you wound me," Preacher said, clutching at his heart. Eva laughed and leaned over to give him a loud, noisy kiss.

"I'll make it all better later," she said, wiggling her eyebrows at him.

Angelina laughed at the couple. It was obvious that they loved each other deeply and their teasing had an affectionate quality to it that she had longed for but never had.

The conversation flowed between the friends as they waited for the food to be served. The guys got up and grabbed drinks for the table, the women opting to hold off on their drinking until after they had eaten. As she waited for her diet coke, she felt like someone was staring at her and she glanced around the room until she saw a woman who looked like she was close to her own age giving her a dirty look. "Eva?"

"Yeah, Angel, what's up?"

"Who is that woman over there? The one in the miniskirt and red shirt?"

"That's Tina, why?"

"She's giving me eat-shit-and-die looks and I know I don't know her."

Eva glanced over to where the woman in question was standing and then said, "She's a friend of one of the Brothers' girlfriends, Sass, I think, and for whatever reason, she had set her sights on Zeke, but he made it clear he wasn't interested. I'm guessing that she has figured out that you're with him seeing as you walked in holding hands and he has had his arm around you since you sat down."

"Well, she'll get over it or I'll have a few words to say to her," Angelina declared.

Renda chuckled hearing Angelina's declaration. "Yeah, sweetie, I remember the last one you had words with," she said.

Angelina rolled her eyes before she said, "She disrespected an old lady, plain and simple. I may not be that here, but I won't be disrespected by anyone ever again. Period."

Zeke and Dex, coming up on the tail end of Angelina's statement, looked at Renda who merely shrugged. "What's going on, you two?" Dex asked.

"Nothing, Dex," Angelina replied. "Just had a question and Eva answered it."

Realizing that she wasn't going to say anything further, Dex let it drop, mainly because the servers were coming around with plates of food. Once everyone was served, Zeke stood and, while holding her hand in his, blessed the meal. Conversation flowed throughout the room and laughter rang out from time to time. Angelina found that she was having a great time and wasn't sure how much of it had to do with the fact that her friends were there for silent moral support. But she was thinking it had more to do with the man sitting to her left. Until they started eating, he had kept an arm around her shoulders and would occasionally toy with one of the curls cascading down her back. *I don't know where this is going, God, but I'm glad You're along for this ride because I don't want to make a mistake again* she thought.

"Cherub?"

"Hmm?"

"You okay? You kind of drifted off somewhere there for a minute."

"I'm sorry. Thinking about how good of a time I'm having," she replied.

"I'm glad. Do you want any dessert?"

"Hmm, no, I've been saving room for the strawberry margaritas that Eva promised me," she told him, trying but failing to keep a serious look on her face.

"Well, there's always room for those," Eva called out from across the table, having heard her last comment. "In fact, if you ladies are ready, we have to man the bar and make them ourselves since they are 'sissy drinks' according to *some* people around here," she said, looking pointedly at Preacher who just grinned at her and raised his beer.

Going to stand up, she was surprised when Zeke tugged her down and gave her a quick kiss, which elicited a few catcalls from some Brothers at the next table. Once again, she felt someone staring at her and when she glanced around, she saw it was that woman again, Tina. She raised her eyebrow at her in a silent challenge as she made her way with Eva, Renda, and Debbie to the bar. Once behind the bar, Eva got down to business, giving each of them a task while she measured out the mix and alcohol. As they mixed up two pitchers, Tina came walking up to the bar and sat down. Eva looked at her and said, "Something I can do for you, Tina?"

"Yeah, I want one of those."

"Well, if you want some, you'll have to get your girl to come behind the bar and make them for you. These are for us."

"Well, *she's* not an old lady," Tina said, pointing at Angelina.

Before Eva could respond, Angelina was standing in front of Tina and she said, "Listen here. You don't know me but I know your type.

You know *nothing* about me at all and for you to say that? Shows your total lack of ignorance regarding this MC. My old man died, bitch, so while I may not be anyone's old lady up here? I most assuredly *am* an old lady of the Heaven's Sinners MC. And can I give you some free advice? If that's what you're looking to become, you may want to try to be less of a bitch to other people because honey? These men don't deal with bitches."

Tina's mouth opened and then closed but nothing came out. Looking at the blonde standing there, now with three women standing at her back who *were* old ladies, had her realizing that saying anything now would be a bad idea. It just galled her that she had been dropping hints at Zeke for quite some time and he had always declined, yet this woman moved into town and had him wrapped around her finger in no time flat. Deciding that the best move was to remove herself, she got up without saying another word and went back to where her friend was sitting. When Sass asked what was going on, she shook her head, not wanting Sass' boyfriend to hear what Angelina had said to her.

Eva looked over at Angelina and said, "Girl, you may be tiny, but you're definitely *not* afraid are you?"

"Oh, I'm afraid of a lot of things, Eva. But women like that? Nope. Not any longer. Been there and done that and while I know I'm not his old lady, I won't have some Brother's girlfriend's friend disrespecting him or any other man who wears a cut in here *or* their old ladies! Now, I need a drink, how about y'all?"

Zeke looked over toward the bar again. He had seen that woman who had been trying to get him to notice her approach the women, seen her say something that had apparently ticked Angelina off and then, after his Cherub said whatever she did, seen her go back to the table she was sitting at without saying another word.

Preacher glanced over at him and said, "I bet, based on the fact that the other three were at her back, she made a comment against either a Brother here or possibly the old ladies. I also can almost guarantee that if we ask, they'll say it was nothing."

"Yeah, Renda and Angel did that all the time and when I would push, one or the other would tell me that just like we have stuff we don't share with them, they have the same in the sisterhood."

About then, the women walked up, frosted glasses and two pitchers of margaritas in hand, along with refills for the men. "We figured that you were due for refills, even if y'all won't fix our drinks," Eva drawled as she handed out the bottles.

Zeke nodded his thanks as he watched Angelina pour herself a drink. Her cheeks looked flushed and her eyes were almost glittery, they were sparkling so much. He leaned over and whispered in her ear, "You okay, Cherub?"

She glanced over her shoulder, not surprised that he was *right there*, and said, "I'm fine, Zeke. Promise."

Taking a sip of her drink, she looked over at Eva and raised her glass saying, "You know what you're doing."

"She should, she's been making them for years," Preacher said.

Eva just rolled her eyes at him as she raised her glass and motioned for the other three women to raise theirs. "To the sisters!"

After clinking glasses, they all finished their first round and quickly refilled their glasses.

Chapter Twelve

As the night wore on, the pitchers of margaritas got stronger and Angelina found she was having the time of her life. One of the Brothers was acting as the DJ and a makeshift dance floor had been put together. She was sitting there tapping her toes when a line dance song came on and Renda looked at her, saying, "C'mon, sweetie, it's time we show our North Georgia family how us 'southern' girls do it!"

Laughing, she put her glass down and headed out to the dance floor, not surprised to find Eva and Debbie and a few other old ladies moving out to line up. It took a few minutes, likely because of the margaritas, before they got into it and before she knew it, they had flowed into a second then a third song. Finally begging off for a drink when the next one started, she headed back to the table. "Cherub? You've got hidden talents," Zeke told her when she sat back down and grabbed her drink. "And I want to dance with you tonight," he whispered next to her ear.

"I'd like that. Zeke? I'm having a great time," she said, looking up at him.

He kissed her forehead and said, "I'm glad, Cherub. I am as well. How much of a headache are you going to have in the morning?"

She giggled as she thought about the drinks she had already had before saying, "Shouldn't be too bad. I'll take something before I go to bed. Just hope I hear the alarm so I don't miss church!"

He chuckled before saying, "I think with the number of folks staying at your house, you'll be okay, yeah?"

The music slowed and he looked at her and held out his hand. "Cherub? Ready to dance?"

"Yes, yes I am."

***

As they watched Zeke and Angelina circle the dance floor, Dex looked over at Preacher and simply said, "He's her kinsman-redeemer, even if he can't see it himself yet."

"Yeah, man. I agree."

Renda, listening in, spoke up and said, "He's going to have to convince *her* though, because she thinks that she shouldn't be an old lady again, she already had that once."

Both men looked at her, incredulous expressions almost identical. "What do you mean, she doesn't think she should be an old lady again? Hell, she's a perfect old lady, and honestly? I can't think of a better woman to stand alongside our President," Preacher said.

"I think she'll get there and I think your President and a lot of prayers from those of us who love her will help her get to that point," Renda stated.

"Yeah, in the meantime, I'm enjoying watching this pan out," Eva said, having come back with another pitcher of the potent margaritas. She topped off all the womens' glasses before she sat back down and continued, "Neither of them realize that what is going on is so far beyond *them*. It's years of prayers being answered. He's more at ease even though he was never really a hard-ass to begin with, and in the short amount of time I've known her, I've seen her blossom."

Debbie looked at her northern sister and said, "You don't know how glad I am that she's building a girl posse up here. That was one thing

I worried about when she left because she's never had a lot of friends until us, but it seems that I worried in vain, huh?"

Eva smiled before she replied. "Yes, you did. She is so kind and her loyalty to this club and her family shines through in everything she says and does."

***

Out on the dance floor and oblivious to their friends' conversation, he held her close while they danced. She loved the feeling of being in his arms; he was respectful but she still knew that he wanted her. As one slow song melted into two, they stayed on the floor. He occasionally kissed her forehead but for the most part, they were content to be in one another's arms.

***

As it got closer to midnight, folks started to leave until only a few remained. Zeke, looking over at Angelina, could tell she was tired and he stood, saying, "I think I need to get my Cherub home."

"Night y'all! Eva, those margaritas are the bomb. Renda? You guys going to be here tomorrow?" Angelina asked as she stood. She was a little wobbly, but overall, didn't feel too rough.

"Yes, we'll be here. See you at the house, yeah?"

"Okay, yeah. Better let your daughter loose, Eva!"

They laughed and Zeke did a general hand wave to the rest of the room before leading her out to his truck. Since he wanted her in the middle, he helped her up on the driver's side and was thrilled to see that she caught the hint as she buckled up in the middle seat. He jumped in and buckled up before he started the truck.

"Zeke?"

"Hmm, Cherub?"

"Thank you for the best night of my life."

"My pleasure, Cherub. I had a great time as well," he said as he headed toward her house.

Once they arrived, she was surprised to see every light on and glanced at him with a worried expression. "I hope everything is okay."

"I'm sure it's fine, Cherub. Let's go in and see for sure, yeah?" he asked as he helped her down.

"Okay."

On the porch, he turned her to him and pulled her into his arms. "C'mere, Cherub," he softly said.

She stood there, his arms around her, wondering why they hadn't gone into the house, when he leaned down and captured her lips in a blistering kiss. Losing herself in his embrace, she kissed him back not caring what that said about her. He was demanding without being overbearing and her heart sang at how he was making her feel. When he finally pulled back, she was breathless. He pressed a quick kiss to her lips before he took her keys and unlocked the door.

***

They found Tally curled up on the couch in the family room, the television on and playing a suspense movie. Seeing that, she figured that the teens had probably watched scary movies, causing her to turn all the lights on. Going over to the teen, she gently shook her awake, saying, "Tally, hon, I'm home."

Tally woke up and smiled up at Angelina. "Hey, did y'all have a good time?"

"We did. How were the girls?"

"They were fantastic. We played outside for a long time after they ate. They really like their playhouse, don't they?"

"Yes, they do, that's for sure!"

"Once I fed them and gave them a bath, we watched Tangled and Frozen and then I put them to bed."

"Thank you again for watching them. I take it Thad and Amelia left already?"

"Yeah, the prospect took them home so she would make curfew."

"And did he ask her?"

"Yes! While I was giving the girls a bath, he asked her to the dance. She said yes!"

Standing, she looked around and then told Angelina, "Sorry about all the lights. We found the scary movie channel and after they left, I felt too alone."

Angelina laughed because if she was honest, she didn't like those kinds of movies and would have done the same thing. As she went to get her purse to pay Tally for the evening, she saw that Zeke already had his wallet out and was handing the teen several twenties. "Zeke? What are you doing?"

"Taking care of Tally, Angelina."

"But…but…"

"No buts about it, Cherub. Our date, my responsibility, yeah?"

She raised an eyebrow at him but didn't say anything else. He finished paying Tally and walked her out to her car. Angelina went to the girls' room and was making sure they were covered when he came into the room. She watched him go over and tuck one of the Cabbage Patch dolls in and smooth a lock of hair back and smiled inside. Placing one last kiss on the sleeping child in front of her, she headed back down the hall.

He caught up with her in the family room where she was straightening up. The teens hadn't left a mess, but he knew she was suddenly nervous being alone around him. Sitting down in the recliner, he motioned for her to come to him and when she did, he pulled her into his lap and got her situated to his liking.

"Zeke? What…what are you doing?"

"Well, traditionally, after a date, when the guy likes the girl, they might make out a for a little while," he told her as he nuzzled along the side of her neck.

"Oh…"

He continued feathering kisses along her neck, taking note of the places where she shivered slightly, before he claimed her lips. Hands now threaded in her hair, something he had wanted to do all night long, he claimed her wholly, letting his lips and tongue show her what he knew she wasn't ready to verbally hear. Yet. Her soft moans had him shifting her closer and he deepened the kiss.

Holy hell she thought. As a variety of emotions flew through her mind, one thing became abundantly clear: he had her whether he knew it or not. A boldness she didn't know she had caused her to reach up and run her hand along his neck and through his hair. *Soft, oh-so-soft* she thought as she kissed him back. She pulled back slightly and lightly nipped his lower lip before laving it with her tongue to soothe the sting.

He groaned low in his throat as he fought to maintain control. *Not like this* he admonished himself. He feathered kisses along her jawline and pulled her earlobe into his mouth to suck on it lightly. As she squirmed in his lap, he realized that she would know how she affected him and some part of his brain rejoiced.

Pulling back, he sighed before he kissed her forehead. "Cherub, as much as I'm enjoying this, I need to go before I can't go, yeah?"

She breathed in deeply before she nodded. "I understand."

Helping her stand, he held her hand as he walked toward the front door. "Make sure you lock up, Cherub, yeah?"

"I will once Dex and Renda get back," she said, grateful that her friends had given them a little bit of privacy.

"Well, at least lock it until they get here, okay?"

She smiled softly before saying, "Okay, Zeke. I'll see you in the morning?"

"Yeah, Cherub. I'll see you in the morning."

Chapter Thirteen

Waking up the next morning before the alarm went off, she was happy to note that she only had a minor headache. *Easy enough to fix* she thought as she got up and showered. If she had timed it right, she had enough time to make something to take for today's potluck as Saturday had been too full. She put on a pot of coffee, knowing that Renda would need at least half of that to feel human judging by her condition when they got in the night before.

As she whipped up a Hummingbird cake, she created a breakfast casserole and slipped it into the oven. While they both baked, she sat at the kitchen table and made out a list for the upcoming week. Hearing a noise, she looked up and saw Dex come into the kitchen. "Good morning, Angel," he said as he kissed the top of her head.

"Good morning to you too. Coffee's ready. Is Renda up yet?"

Dex, busy fixing his first cup, looked at her before saying, "Uh, not really. She's moving a little bit slow this morning."

"I bet she is! It was a lot of fun last night, wasn't it?" she asked, getting up to check on the casserole. Seeing it was done, she pulled it out to cool, and set the timer for the cake before she made the frosting.

"Yeah, it was, Angel. Their parties are as crazy as ours are, too," he replied, sipping on his coffee. "Do you know the meaning of the word 'relax'?"

"I am relaxing, you goof! But I didn't have time yesterday to make something for today and I woke up early enough to make sure that I could take care of that this morning. Once the cake is out and cooling, I'll get the girls up and fed and even with taking the time to frost the cake, we should still make it to church on time."

"Let me take some of this into Renda and see if I can get her moving so she can give you a hand, yeah?"

"She needs to get moving, but I'm good. I've got this, Dex, I promise," she told him.

***

Each week, the sermons got better she thought as she prepared to get the girls from the nursery. Feeling a hand at the small of her back, she glanced up and saw Zeke standing there. "You going to get the girls, Cherub?"

"Yeah. I brought them clothes to change into since Eva mentioned something about water guns and balloons. What is that about?"

"On the first hot day, we usually let the kids have a bit of fun with both," he told her as he took her hand.

"Ah, I see. What about us adults?"

"We occasionally get hit, but we're supposed to be off-limits," he replied.

After collecting the girls, he helped her get them into her SUV then kissed her quickly before saying, "I'll see you there, okay Cherub? I'm on grill duty today and need to get a move on."

"Oh! You should have said something, you didn't need to help me," she said to him.

"I never do anything I don't want to do, Cherub, yeah?" he told her, brushing his fingers down her cheek. "Now, I'll see you there. Do the girls prefer hotdogs or hamburgers?"

She started laughing and then said, "Mellie likes hotdogs but Cailyn prefers hamburgers."

"I'll make sure there are plenty made so they don't have to wait long."

"See you there, Zeke. Be careful," she said, noticing that he was on his bike. She wondered if she would ever be behind him on his bike, then shook her head for her wishful thinking.

✻✻✻

With lunch now over, the adults sat in the "water free zone" and watched the kids run around, tossing water balloons and using super soakers on one another. Conversation was, as always, free-flowing. Angelina looked for Eva and seeing her, waved her over. "Hey, Eva, I know y'all met last night, but Debbie owns the salon down in South Georgia. She's the reason I know even a smidgen of what I know about your industry." The two women started talking and Eva told Debbie about their pending trip to Premiere Orlando, which had Angelina hollering for Dex. "Dex? Listen, we started paying for the stylists' trips to these continuing education seminars, do you want to do the same for Debbie and her girls that want to attend?"

"Whatever you think is best, Angel," Dex replied. "If it helps them, it will help us, right?"

"Right. Okay then, Debbie? You want to check with your stylists and let me know how many want to go so I can coordinate everything? I wasn't sure if Dex would go for it, but I've got a block of rooms pre-booked and only need to confirm the reservation for those and I also need to buy the tickets. I figured the Heaven's Sinners folks would want to be together, will that work?"

Both Eva and Debbie looked at her before Debbie said, "Girl, this has me so excited I can't wait to tell the rest of them! And Eva said she's liking the new inventory system."

"Yeah, I figure it will take a month or two to iron anything out, but we should start seeing a positive upswing soon. Plus, I found some great sets that will work the closer we get to the holidays."

Eva started laughing. "Angel, we haven't even hit *summer* yet!"

"I know, I know, but I want to be prepared so that both locations do a bang-up business. I have a few other ideas as well, but will run them by Zeke and Dex before I share them, okay?"

"Are you talking shop?" Zeke asked, coming up behind her. "What did I say about Sunday being a day of rest?"

"I wasn't working, I was merely sharing some needed information," she informed him. Without warning, he scooped her up and headed toward where the kids were still playing, eliciting shrieks and giggles as she started getting soaked from the water balloons. Seeing Tally and Thad, with a shyly smiling Amelia next to him, holding super soakers, she said, "Zeke! Don't you…oh my word!" Totally drenched now, she glared at him because the three teens had bombarded her with their super soakers. "Just look at me!"

He looked down at the woman in his arms, hair dripping wet, make-up running, T-shirt soaked and plastered to her body, and said, "My beautiful hot mess," before he kissed her.

How can I stay mad when he says shit like that she thought, returning the kiss before little girl giggles reached her ears. Pulling back, she saw Melora and Cailyn standing there watching him kiss her. "Zeke, the girls!" she hissed into his ear.

He smiled down at the two little girls before he leaned back in and said, "Cherub, nothing wrong with them seeing someone being affectionate with their Momma." Putting her down, he reached for Melora and swung her up in his arms causing the little girl to burst into giggles. Cailyn, still a bit shy, watched her sister until he put her down and scooped her up. She liked him, he made her Momma smile a lot and was always doing fun things with and for them. As Zeke played with the girls, Angelina tried to sneak away to get changed, but he spotted her and giving the little one in his arms a quick kiss and putting her down, he reached out and grabbed her hand, pulling her toward him.

"Zeke, what are you doing now? I was going to see if I could find something drier, I can't sit out here like this," she said while her arm did a Vanna-like sweep down the front of her.

He grinned, she painted a beautiful picture, standing there with a wet T-shirt, hair that was equal parts wet and dry and of course, what make-up she had on now smeared. Reaching out, he ran a finger across her cheek before he leaned in and said, "Want some help with that, Cherub?"

He watched as a blush stole across her cheeks and then said, "As much as I would love to do just that, my Cherub, don't think now is the time or the place. But I will take you to my room so you can clean up and change, yeah?"

Still stuck on his earlier comment which had sent her mind off on a whirlwind of thoughts, she merely nodded and let him lead her into the clubhouse and down to his room. Once there, he grabbed her one of his T-shirts and told her he would be waiting outside until she was done. Looking in the mirror, she saw that she was beyond a hot mess and set about repairing the damage.

Twenty minutes later, face scrubbed free of make-up and hair now braided, she walked out of the bathroom in his dry T-shirt and a pair of capris she had tossed into the girls' bag. Her bra was still damp but she didn't think it would be enough to wet his shirt, which was huge on her. She stopped short when she saw him lounging on the bed, back against the headboard. He motioned for her and she found herself next to the bed before she knew what was happening. "Zeke?"

"Hmm, Cherub?" he asked as he pulled her down next to him and then worked to arrange her how he wanted.

"What…what are you doing?"

"Well, I have the girls laying down in Preacher and Eva's room, so I thought we could take a Sunday nap as well."

"Together?"

"Yeah, Cherub, together. You okay with that?" he asked as he pulled a cover over her.

"Uh…well, no one is going to think anything about it, are they?"

He glanced at her face and saw the worry written there. "No, Cherub, no one is going to say or think anything. I've set the alarm but Eva said she'd keep an ear out for the girls, okay?"

"Okay, Zeke. I trust you."

I trust you. Three words that resonated deep in his soul. This woman, whose full story he still didn't know nor did he care if he ever did *trusted* him and that said more to him than if she had uttered declarations of undying love.

He cradled her face in his hands and kissed her, being careful not to get things stirred up too much. After all, he was looking at forever, eventually, so he could afford to be patient now. Ending the kiss, he again got her comfortable before he said, "Now sleep, Cherub. This is one of the best parts of Sunday, a nap."

***

Waking up in his arms was a delicious feeling she thought. Tilting her head back, she could see his profile. He had fallen asleep with his arms surrounding her and his head turned toward her. She reached up and smoothed back the hair that had fallen over his brow and was surprised when his eyes opened and he smiled. "Hey Cherub," he said, voice raspy with sleep. "You sleep okay?"

"I did, yes. I kind of like the idea of a Sunday nap."

"Me too. I especially like them when you're in my arms."

She shook her head a little and he reached up to cup her jaw and tilt her head back so she could see him. "I'm serious, Cherub. Best two-hour nap I think I've ever had. Want to go see if the girls are back up?"

She didn't know what came over her, but seeing him and being warm and cuddled up against him, she reached up and kissed him. What started out as an innocent peck on the lips quickly turned into a passionate, no-holds-barred kiss and before she knew it, she was on her back and he was half laying across her, his hands running along her sides as he kissed her.

She's going to be the death of me, Lord he thought as he struggled to regain control. He pulled back slowly, kissing her cheeks, her forehead, the side of her neck where her pulse was rapidly beating. "Cherub?"

"Hmm?"

"We need to get up before we can't get up," he told her as he sat up and pulled her up alongside him.

"I...I guess."

"But I want you to know, someday, when the time is right, we won't be getting up, yeah?"

***

Back outside with everyone, the girls ran down to the playground and she sat with the old ladies, somewhat surprised that Sass was there. She raised an eyebrow at Eva and nodded in Sass' direction, which prompted her friend to say, "Butch asked her to be his old lady last night."

"Sass that's awesome!" Angelina said.

Sass looked over at Angelina and a light blush came over her face. "Uh, Angelina?"

"Yeah, babe."

"I owe you an apology."

"For what?"

"For how Tina was acting last night. I should have known the only reason she befriended me was that she was trying to become an old lady. Butch had told me that's what he had heard, but I didn't want to believe it. I'm sorry for whatever she said last night."

"Not your apology to make, babe. It's all good, yeah? She'll never become an old lady going from Brother to Brother and especially not if she chooses to act like a bitch toward other old ladies."

"Yeah, I don't think she'll be coming around any longer. She said some things last night after you left that made me angry and I don't like how she's done some of the Brothers."

"Well, you have us," Marta said, having come in on the tail end of the conversation. "And we rock, right? In fact, we need an old ladies' night out to bring you into the fold."

Angelina smiled. She remembered those girl's nights fondly, even though Laser had always instigated a fight either right before or when she got home. "You'll have a great time, Sass," she told the new old lady.

Eva spoke up and said, "Uh, you'll be coming with, Angel."

"Newsflash, girlfriend, I'm no longer an old lady."

"Once an old lady, always an old lady," the other woman said. "Besides, I'm thinking that status is going to change if what I think is happening is actually happening."

Angelina rolled her eyes at her friend. "Whatevs. Fine, I'll go, but only because I need a girl's night out, okay?"

As the women continued to talk, Renda and Debbie looked at one another and smiled. Their girl was finding her way and adding to her posse. They felt no jealousy, knowing that whenever they were up visiting, they would be enfolded in the group as if they lived there.

"So, Angel, what's going on between you and Zeke?" Marta asked.

Angelina glanced at the group of women and saw every eye was on hers. "Uh…can I plead the fifth?"

Cries of "no" chorused throughout the women. Realizing she wasn't getting out of it, she finally gave in, saying, "He's told me he's interested and that he's been praying for God's will in all of it. We spend a lot of time together, mostly for the businesses, but last night was our first date."

"And?"

"And I had a marvelous time. He brought me flowers and has been great with the girls."

"Girl, I think what I said earlier on is coming to pass; he's your kinsman-redeemer."

"Too soon. It's too soon."

"You know that His timing is perfect. Not too late and not too soon. Just roll with it, yeah? I've never seen him like this and it looks good on him," Eva said.

Chapter Fourteen

Two Months Later

As spring slid into summer, Angelina found herself with extra time on her hands since the books were current and everything was running smoothly with the inventory sheets she had put into place. She smiled thinking about the upcoming week-they were leaving on the family run the next day and she had a lot to get together.

While she worked in the kitchen baking brownies and cookies, her mind drifted to Zeke. Since their first date, he had taken her out weekly. Sometimes with a group of Brothers and their old ladies, sometimes just the two of them. They still did their breakfast meetings twice a week, but now spent more time talking than going over anything. All the businesses were thriving and he had just received the check from the prosecutor's office for the monies the accountant had stolen. Even though the trial still pended, because the prosecutor had all the needed information, the monies were released. She smiled thinking of how the Brothers were going to react next week. Zeke had her cut the checks for their portion of the monies and they were going to be ecstatic with the amounts. He still popped over frequently, sometimes with food and sometimes, to take her and the girls out. And the girls? They adored him and his open affection toward the both of them had them blossoming further. Thad also spent a lot of time at her house. Sometimes to do something his dad asked him to take care of, like cut the grass. Other times, he would bring Amelia over.

Thoughts of Thad and Amelia had her laughing quietly. She remembered when she overheard him tell his dad that he didn't know how to dance. Not thinking twice about it, she had pushed the furniture back and queued up a music station on her television and then she had proceeded to teach him how to dance. For the slow dances, Zeke assisted, showing his son through his actions how to respect the young woman he wanted to date. It had been a fun-filled night, especially when the girls joined in, because both Zeke and Thad danced with them. She wanted that for her girls; a solid man who would love them so that they would know how to be treated properly. The best part was when Thad brought Amelia over to see her before they left for the dance. She had taken some pictures of the two of them, as well as Tally and her date since the foursome were riding together.

She smiled contentedly. *Thank You God for these many blessings* she thought. Her house was a home and people felt welcome in it, something she had always wanted since leaving the Cooks all those years ago. The only wrinkle in her life was the fact that she hadn't told Zeke everything. She knew he had said he didn't care, but she wanted him to know. Tonight, she reasoned with herself. I'll tell him tonight.

***

The girls finally settled for the night, she returned to the family room where Zeke was waiting, a bowl of popcorn and two sodas on the end table beside him. "C'mere, Cherub," he said to her as she walked into the room. *I love our movie nights* she thought.

As she got comfortable on his lap, she said, "Can we talk, Zeke?"

"Yeah, Cherub. What do you want to talk about?"

Seeing the slight unease cross her face, he mentally braced himself for whatever she was going to say and sent up a silent prayer as well. He leaned over and kissed her forehead, saying, "You know you don't have to tell me anything, Cherub. Or you can tell me everything. Regardless, it won't change how I feel."

She drew in a deep breath before she exhaled quickly. "No, I think you need to know this but it's hard to know where to start."

"The beginning's always a good place," he said softly.

"Okay, well you know how Dex and Laser found me and rescued me from the streets already so I won't cover old history. Dex has always been a straight-shooter around me. Laser was his best friend, but apparently he had a shitty home life and it colored everything. He never beat me- physically, anyway- but his words were just as cutting and hurtful and it played hell on my mind for a long time. It was almost as if, whenever things were going well that he would deliberately sabotage it by making an ugly comment. Sometimes he did it in front of Brothers but never when Dex was around because I think he would have hurt him.

Anyhow, he wasn't faithful to me, not by a long-shot. Because of that, I always insisted that he wear protection, but I still ended up with an infection he gave me. The doctors got it cleared up, but it put a wedge between us, one I couldn't get past. You see, the doctors said I most likely would never get pregnant because the infection caused some damage inside. The night he died, it…it had been months since he had touched me. The fact that I got pregnant, to me, was a miracle. I…I just wanted you to know because I probably can't have any more kids."

He sat silently while she talked, occasionally rubbing her back or smoothing her hair. As precious as this woman had become to him, he couldn't fathom the fact that she had been treated so callously and by a Brother at that. He pulled her closer and placed a kiss on her temple then said, "Cherub, I'm sorry. You shouldn't have had to go through any of that at all. I'm glad you told me, but like I said, it doesn't change how I feel about you one bit. Whether you can have a hundred kids or not is irrelevant to me, yeah?"

Hearing the sincerity in his words, she felt herself relax. In every way, he had shown her the depth of his affection. He treated her with respect and as if she mattered, and she felt cherished whenever he was around. Reaching up to run her hand along the side of his jaw, she looked at him and said, "I love you, Zeke. More than words can express. More than I ever thought possible. And I thank God every day for bringing me here."

Before he claimed her lips with his own, he whispered, "And I love and adore you, my Cherub."

The movie forgotten, they spent some time "necking" as Zeke called it, until he once again called a halt. She let out a frustrated sigh before asking him, "When, Zeke?"

"Soon, Cherub."

"Is that your final answer?"

He started chuckling at her use of a catch-phrase from a popular game show. "Yeah, Cherub, at least for right now." He helped her up and she walked him to the door, where he kissed her again before saying, "I'll be here in the morning to help you round up the girls and get them fed. Then, you're riding with me."

Oh my word she thought. *I love when he uses that voice.* "Okay, Zeke. It's been awhile since I've been on a bike, though."

"It'll come back to you, Cherub. Now be sure to lock up, yeah?"

"Yeah, Zeke, I will."

"Love you, Cherub. I'll see you bright and early."

"Love you too, Zeke."

Chapter Fifteen

She was running around like a chicken with her head cut off making sure she had everything for the girls, as well as herself, when the doorbell rang. Running to the door, she opened it to a smiling Zeke. "Good morning, Cherub," he said, coming inside and then giving her a kiss.

"Morning, Zeke. I'm not quite ready yet. We had another breakfast episode which resulted in an unscheduled bath. I'm sorry," she told him, already heading back down to her room.

He followed her and once inside said, "Cherub? What can I do to help? Thad was following me so I can have him load things up and give you a hand."

"Uh, well, I have containers with baked goodies in the kitchen, and platters of sandwiches in the fridge. I've pulled out drinks for the girls and myself, and I also have my share of the stuff needed for margaritas. It's all on the kitchen table except the sandwiches. Oh! And since I know he's got to run, I have Gatorade for Thad, make sure he grabs that and the two cases of water."

"Just to say, Cherub, there *are* stores up where we're going, yeah?"

"I know, but I was out and about and grabbed it so we don't have to stop having fun."

He shook his head at her logical thinking-they would have sent a prospect if anything was needed, and most likely would still do so. He asked again, "Cherub? What can I do to help?"

"Well, I have my stuff almost packed, the girls *are* packed, so not too much other than keep me company?"

"I can do that. Do you have just a minute before you go hunting for more clothes?" he asked her.

She stopped pulling out nightgowns and looked at him. He had a serious look on his face and her insides clenched. Not realizing that she wore her emotions so well, she was somewhat surprised when he reached out and tucked some hair behind her ear before he led her over to her sitting area. As he sat down, he pulled her into his lap. "Cherub? Got an important question to ask, yeah?"

"Um, okay…"

"I want you to be my old lady, especially since you're riding on the back of my bike for this run."

"Was that a question or a statement?" she asked him, smiling slightly.

He chuckled before kissing her and said, "Cherub, would you be my old lady?"

"Yes, Zeke, I would be honored to be alongside you as your old lady," she told him as she reached out to kiss him.

Before things got too heated, *again,* she thought, he pulled back and helped her back up, patting her lightly as he told her he would be right back. She went back to her dresser and pulled out different nightwear-if she was now his old lady, she didn't want him seeing her in ratty nightgowns!

He went back out to his truck and grabbed the cut he had for her, taking it into the house. His bike was at the clubhouse, and there was a prospect coming with Thad to load up her stuff. Smiling to himself, he thought of the other things he had in his saddlebags. Months together spent talking, plus the insight that Dex had provided, had him knowing that she wouldn't expect anything beyond being an old lady. But he wanted more and planned to ask her another important question while they were gone.

Back inside, he saw her dragging her small suitcase down the hall and went to help her, putting it by the front door. He then went into the girls' room and grabbed their bag and babies, along with their sunglasses and little hats, and put those by the door as well.

Listening, he heard her in the kitchen and he went to find her and had to stop to catch his breath. She was bent over, searching the refrigerator, and he was stunned to find himself reacting. "Cherub, like the picture you're presenting right now."

She turned quickly at his words and he was amused to see her flush. "Zeke!" she hissed, "You can't say that kind of thing where Thad could hear!"

He glanced out the back window and saw Thad and the prospect had arrived and were out with the girls at their playhouse. "Thinking we're good, Cherub. C'mere."

She went willingly into his arms, looping her arms around his waist right before he lowered his lips to hers. As all rational thought left her once again, she reveled in how he made her feel. He continued to kiss her, eventually pulling back enough to look at her dazed eyes before he said, "Love you, Cherub. What say we get this show on the road?"

How can he talk much less function after that she thought as she worked to make her limbs move. Going to the back door, she called the kids in and then went to pull the platters of sandwiches out of the fridge. Once the kids came in, she made sure the door was locked and deadbolted then turned to Thad and said, "Your dad said you would load things up for the trip. Most of it is by the front door, but this needs to go too."

"That's cool, Angelina. Yeah, I've got it," he replied, grabbing the containers of the baked goodies.

Before long everything was loaded and she was checking to make sure nothing was left behind. Waiting by the door, Zeke finally said, "Cherub, if we forgot something, we'll send a prospect to get it, okay?"

"Okay. I'm ready to go anyhow and am sure I got all the girls will need," she replied, walking up to where he was waiting.

"Just one thing, Cherub. You'll need this," he said, as he lifted the cut from behind his back to help her put it on. She looked and saw his property patch on the back but on the front, he had put "Zeke's Cherub" over the left breast pocket and "Angel" was over the right. Once he had it on her, he kissed her nose and putting his hand on her low back, led her out the door and to his truck.

***

Things seemed to happen fast once they got to the clubhouse. Vehicles were loaded, kids were with assigned people who were driving, and the men and women riding bikes were busy getting helmets and gloves on. Zeke walked over to where Angelina was standing with Eva and Marta and motioned for her to turn around. She did so and felt his hands in her hair, braiding it before he tucked it underneath her cut. When he spun her around again, she laughed because he had found her a pink bandana and was busy getting that around her hair before he handed her a helmet.

"Zeke? You know I've ridden before, yeah?" she finally asked him.

"I know, Cherub, but you're the only old lady I've had so humor me, okay? I need to do this to make sure you're as protected as I can make you."

Her heart melted hearing him say that-she knew he had been married before, but they had split up before he joined the MC so she had never been his old lady. Knowing that she was going to be his first and only? Priceless. She reached out a hand to stop him, saying, "Zeke, I love you for what you're doing to take care of me. You show me every day, in some way, that I matter to you, and that means a lot."

He kissed her nose and led her over to his bike. When he got on and tipped for her to get on behind him, she felt a shiver run up her spine. Sure, they had cuddled and done a lot of kissing, but most of the time, they weren't as close as they would be while riding.

***

They stopped halfway for lunch at a diner they frequented whenever they did this run. The owner remembered them and always had a word or three to say to the guys and their old ladies. And she spoiled the teens and little ones. When she saw Zeke carrying Melora while guiding Angelina in as she carried Cailyn, she broke out into a wide grin and said, "I have been hoping you'd find your special one, Zeke! How's Thad? Did he come with you this time around? Who are these two cuties?"

"Gloria, this is Angelina, my old lady and these two are Melora and Cailyn, her little girls. Thad is somewhere with Tally, because she brought her best friend, Amelia, who Thad is seeing."

"Pleased to meet you, Angelina. Do these little ones like strawberry milk or chocolate milk better?"

Angelina began laughing. Once she calmed, she said, "One of each, please. They may be twins but they definitely have different likes when it comes to the way they like their milk!"

"Get it right away. Zeke? What about y'all?"

"Sweet tea for me and Diet Coke for my Cherub."

As Gloria turned away, she smiled at his use of cherub. *This one is definitely special, Lord. Glad to see he found her.*

They didn't linger long over lunch, wanting to get to the cabins and settled in so they could relax. As they left, Zeke made sure to hand Gloria some extra money beyond what they all tipped, saying, "Take care of those animals I see you're still feeding, yeah?"

"Thanks, Zeke. Got them all spayed and neutered and up-to-date on their shots, now building a barn so they have somewhere out of the elements. Quite a few of the younger ones have found homes, but the ones left are older and folks don't always want them, y'know?"

He nodded because he understood. Then he wondered how his Cherub would feel if they got a few on their way back. "Got anything gentle? Would be good with kids?" he asked Gloria.

"I might, yeah."

"When we stop back, want to take a look, yeah? Thinking two little girls would love to have a kitty or two to spoil and because my Cherub has her office at home, they'll get plenty of attention."

"Works for me, Zeke. Y'all enjoy yourselves and keep the wheels straight."

He reached down and gave the woman a hug. She had been feeding them for years, never looked down on them for being bikers, and even mentioned once that she prayed for their safety when they were out on runs. She was also running a rescue, and he wasn't sure how she managed to do that plus run a business. He made a mental note to get her information when they came back through so he could have Angelina send her money every month to further her efforts.

***

"Zeke, this place is gorgeous!" Angelina said, wonder in her tone.

"It's got five master bedrooms and then a room down in the basement set up with bunkbeds. We generally put the kids down there, and Marta and her old man, Pudge, stay in that room to keep an eye and ear out and make sure the teens aren't up to no good."

"Wow. Well, she has a way with kids and I know the girls adore her. Plus, her daughters are here and the four of them have become thicker than thieves!"

He grinned at her as he led her to his room. What she didn't know was the MC owned the property and the cabins, occasionally renting them out to other MCs for retreats and such. Whenever they made the call to come up for a family week, a couple of prospects went up a day or two early and stocked the place and aired it out and made sure it was clean. He stopped in front of his door and unlocked it before he scooped her up, bridal style, and carried her across the threshold.

"Zeke? What are you doing?"

"Hmmm, just showing my old lady what she means to me," he replied as he carefully set her down. His bags had been brought in already and he went over to the bigger one and pulled out some Epsom salts. "Thought you might want to soak since it's been a bit since you've been on a bike."

She blushed a little because she *was* sore, but not in the way she wanted to be. "Thank you, handsome. I think I'll take advantage of a soak if the kids are okay?"

"Cherub, the teens and prospects have *all* the kids to give the parents a chance to be alone," he told her as he put his clothes away.

"Ah, I see," she replied, her voice muffled as she was searching through her bag for a pair of capris and a tank top.

She didn't know it but while she soaked, he planned to take a quick shower to wash off the road grime. He grinned to himself as he took his stuff into the bathroom and headed into the shower section. He was impressed with how the builder had designed each bathroom, the shower stall was huge but separate from the bathtub. He was already under the water soaping himself when he heard her go into where the tub was located and his body started to react to the sheer proximity. Knowing she was disrobing and climbing into a tub, he debated the wisdom of taking matters into his own hand. *Not happening* he thought, pulling on the self-control he was known for as he quickly finished his shower and dressed before he stood outside the bathing chamber and said, "Cherub? I'll see you when you're done, yeah? Want anything to drink?"

Laying in a tub filled with hot water that had her skin rosy, she thought about Zeke. She wondered how it would be when they finally had sex-would he be more focused on his needs and wants? Sighing, she sent up a quick prayer that they would be compatible, at least. He was considerate, respectful and loving and treated her in a way that made her feel cherished. If it didn't extend to physical intimacy, she would be grateful for what she *did* have with him. Finished with her bath, she got out and dried and grabbed her brush to work out the tangles. Even braided and under her cut, she had managed to end up with quasi-Medusa hair.

Back out in the bedroom, she found Zeke lounging on the bed, remote control in his hand as he channel hopped. Settling on a football game, he motioned for her to join him and she climbed onto the bed next to him. A squeal of surprise escaped her lips when he lifted her to put her between his legs, taking the brush out of her hand. "What are you doing?" she finally asked.

"Gonna brush your hair for you, Cherub," he said as he worked the brush slowly through the cascading curls.

She let her head fall forward, this was an unexpected treat and he was so gentle as he worked through the tangles the trip and her bath had left behind, occasionally dropping a kiss alongside her neck. Once he was done, his hands returned to her hair and he pulled it together in one hand and laid it so it draped down along the front of her before he began massaging her neck and shoulders. She moaned at how he seemed to instinctively know where to press harder and where to smooth. "Feel good, Cherub?" he asked as he leaned in to nuzzle her neck before he nipped gently.

"Mmhmm," she replied as he moved down her back easing muscles she didn't even know were tight. *Shit if he kept this up, she was going to be nothing but a puddle of goo* she thought. Her body was reacting to his touch and she blushed slightly at where her thoughts were going. *It must be the unknown* she thought as his hands made their way under her shirt while he continued to caress and massage her.

Silk he thought. *Soft, silky skin.* He couldn't wait to taste her, to make her his, but he could tell she had some hesitancy. Unsure of how to ask her in a way that wouldn't upset her, he continued what he was doing. He suspected it had to do with her past experiences with Laser and he didn't want anyone else in their bed. Wrapping his arms around her waist, he drew her back before he lifted a hand and turned her head so he could kiss her. As he nibbled and kissed, he felt her relax slightly and knew that his earlier suspicions had likely been correct. His Brother hadn't taken care of her, something he planned to do as often as feasibly possible. Turning her in his arms so she was cradled against his shoulder, he continued kissing her even as one of hands began gently stroking along her side. He heard her breath catch when he stroked along her breast and felt her squirm a bit in his lap, something that made him even harder, if that was possible.

"Cherub?" he whispered in her ear before sucking the earlobe into his mouth.

"Hmm?"

"Want you, but only if you're okay with it, yeah?" It would kill him, but he figured that was one of the reasons God had invented cold water.

She opened her eyes and gazed up at him. Her eyes were at half-mast and he knew she was likely feeling things she hadn't in a very long time. "Zeke, if you stop, I might go mad," she told him.

"Well, we can't have that now, can we?" he asked as he scooted them down onto the bed so that he was half laying over her. He closed his eyes for a brief moment, inhaling her intoxicating scent that was all her, lightly floral. Leaning in again, he cupped her face and forehead to forehead, looked into her eyes and softly said, "Love you Cherub. Love you so much. Want to make this good for you so you be sure and tell me if there's something I do that you don't like, yeah?"

Stroking his face, feeling his strong jawline beneath his neatly trimmed beard, she responded, saying, "I will, Zeke, promise."

Leaning back, he removed his T-shirt before he carefully took hers off. Clad in a lacy bra and her capris, he couldn't remember ever seeing anything so beautiful. His fingers traced wherever his eyes looked and he was pleased to see her nipples pebbling beneath the fabric. Carefully, he reached behind her and unclasped her bra before he drew the straps down her arm and tossed it over his shoulder. "Beautiful, Cherub. Fucking beautiful," he told her, seeing the rapid rise and fall of her chest as the pulse in her throat jumped. He lightly stroked across her nipple before leaning down and capturing it in his mouth.

Oh my God she thought as his action caused a flood of need to soak her panties. Why on earth had she been worried again? He continued to suckle her breast while his other hand stroked the one he wasn't sucking on, before he switched his attention to the other nipple, paying it the same attention he had the first. She couldn't figure out what to do with her hands, they wanted to clasp his head to her breasts because the feelings were so overwhelming, but they also wanted to touch him. The need to touch him won and he soon felt her small hands moving across his shoulders, running through his hair, stroking down his arms. He gently bit her nipple before soothing it with his lips and tongue, pleased to hear the moans coming from her.

Moving his hand downward while he continued to kiss and lick and nibble her collarbone, her breasts, her jaw, he squeezed her hip and then stroked along her back before cupping her ass. "Zeke," she moaned as she moved restlessly against the pillow.

"Shhh, Cherub," he whispered as he raised up and took her mouth again, kissing her with an almost desperate passion. As he sat back and looked at the picture she made with her hair all over the pillow and her lips and nipples a bright rosy red, he reached down and began to remove her capris, grateful that they had no buttons or zippers to get through because he wasn't sure his hands would cooperate. He saw the flush start across her chest and move into her cheeks when she realized she was laying there exposed to his gaze and he reached out and almost reverently, he touched her face. Rolling away long enough to remove his lounge pants, he rolled back over and took her into his arms so they were on their sides facing one another.

"Ah Cherub, you're stunning. I pray you're ready for me because I don't know how much longer I can wait," he told her, even as one hand ran down to her hip to dip inward to stroke between her thighs. She was ready, more than ready if the truth were told. She moaned as his fingers found their way between her legs and began to stroke her with teasing brushes against her clit. Bringing his fingers to his lips, he watched her as he stuck them in his mouth and sucked them clean. "Delicious, Cherub, and I intend to explore that fact later, yeah?" he told her as he rolled her onto her back and spread her legs. Carefully, because he knew it had been a while for her, he entered her a little at a time, watching her as she adjusted to him. Finally seated balls deep, he rested his forearms along the side of her head and leaned down to take her mouth in a searing kiss. As he began to move, he watched her and was secretly thrilled when she wrapped her legs around his waist even as she pulled his head down and began kissing him with an almost desperate need.

Soft moans and mewls let him know she was close and he reached between them, finding her clit and gently rubbing it in a circular motion as his thrusts grew stronger. "Zeke," she moaned. "I...I'm..."

"Let go, my sweet Cherub, I want to feel you milking me as you come," he told her before he buried his head in the crook of her neck and sucked. As she shattered beneath him, calling out his name, he tried to hold on but feeling how tight she was and how she was gripping him in her warm, slick heat, had him coming a few short strokes later. Just before his strength left him, he rolled them so she was laying on top of him, still connected with the aftershocks of her orgasm coursing through her body.

Gentle kisses across her face and jaw, nose and forehead. She finally came back to her senses and saw him watching her closely. "You okay, Cherub?" he asked her, hands lovingly stroking her body.

The smile that lit up her face had him drawing in another sharp breath. She was almost luminous in the afterglow of their lovemaking and the man inside of him felt a smugness that he knew wasn't right, but he couldn't make himself give a shit. "Never better, Zeke. I…I…well, hell. I had no idea it could be that good. I mean, I don't want to bring ghosts in here with us, y'know? But it wasn't always good for me, so I was kind of nervous about us. You and me."

Finally. She had finally let go enough to let him see what her fear was. "Kind of guessed, Cherub, and no I don't want ghosts here either so we'll talk more later when we're up and dressed, yeah? But I want you to know it's never been this good for me. Ever."

Her Cheshire cat grin had him smiling back at her. Smacking her lightly on the ass, he said,

"What say we get cleaned up and nap for a bit now, yeah?"

***

She woke up from their nap with a smile on her lips. He had been true to his word and they had cleaned up, but not before he taught her the joys of shower sex. As she wiggled back, she felt his arm tighten around her waist before his voice, raspy from sleep, whispered, "Cherub? We have to get up, yeah? You keep moving like that and we won't be getting up for a bit."

Glancing over her shoulder at him, she grinned and then wiggled out from underneath his arm and said, "Thinking everyone knows why we've been holed up since we got here, Zeke."

"Probably, but your old man needs food sustenance for later, yeah?"

With a mock sigh, she leaned down and gave him a quick kiss on the lips before she got up and started hunting the clothes he had tossed willy-nilly hours ago. Now dressed, she went into the bathroom and found a hair tie so she could get her hair pulled up. Finished, she came back out into the bedroom and saw he had already headed toward the kitchen.

***

"Mmmhmm, girl, how was your nap?" Eva asked, a smile in her voice.

"Uh, it was good."

"Just good?" Marta asked, having come in from the outside freezer with stuff to make for dinner.

Now blushing, she looked at her two friends and said, "Much, much better than good. Didn't know it could be like that, to be honest."

Eva gave her a quick hug as she headed toward the stove to stir the potatoes and pasta they would be putting together for salads. "Beyond happy for you, Angel. He's a great guy."

She smiled. Yeah, he was a great guy. Looking out the window, she started laughing. While the women in this house were working on side dishes to go with what the men were grilling, the men had the kids outside and were trying to organize a game of some sort. She noticed Cailyn standing off to the side, not participating, just watching. Melora on the other hand? Fully involved.

"So other than potato and pasta salad, what are we having?" she asked Eva.

"The other old ladies are making baked beans and roasted corn. I think we're supposed to put together a cucumber and onion and tomato salad as well."

She grabbed the items needed for that and set to work. As the three women bustled around the kitchen making tea and lemonade, they kept up a running conversation. Sometimes it veered off tangent, but she didn't care. Once they got the salads put together and in the fridge, they headed outside with drinks for the kids, both big and small, and sat down to watch the antics.

Chapter Sixteen

"Thad?"

"Yeah, Dad?"

"Got a minute?"

Thad looked over at his dad before nodding. They separated from the group and found some shade where they both sat against the tree. "What's up, Dad?"

"I've got a few things I wanted to talk to you about, yeah?"

"Okay. Am I in trouble or something?"

"Nope. Not yet, anyhow. Okay, first, I know you and Amelia are seeing one another. Make sure you are always respecting her, Son. Don't push for things that neither of you are ready to handle. I remember how it was at your age when hormones rule, but she's a good girl and deserves to be cherished, y'hear me?"

Thad nodded. His dad didn't know it, but he had watched how he treated others, especially women, over the years and while his *body* wanted Amelia, he wouldn't let it get past the point of no return. He didn't say anything, but he knew she was the one, even at his age, and he was going to show her the respect she deserved. "Dad, been watching all my life how you treat others, and how Preacher treats his old lady and all the other Brothers too. Not gonna disrespect Amelia."

Zeke smiled inside, glad that lifelong lessons were showing fruit. He nodded, not saying any more, then said, "Now, about Angelina."

Brought back to the conversation at hand by what his dad said, he looked at him and said, "What about her?"

"Planning to ask her to marry me, but only if you're okay with it," his dad finally said.

Thad thought about the woman who had come into his life through his dad. She was warm, loving, generous, and kind, and while she offered advice like a mother would, she hadn't done what a lot of his friends had said happened to them; she didn't go overboard in her attempts to make him like her. He liked how his dad had changed since she came into his life, too. He had always been a good dad, but now? He seemed even more in tune with the things going on around him. Finally, he looked at his dad and said, "Dad, I'm good with it, yeah? She's good for you, for us, and I think she's an answer to prayers that have been said for years. I know you love her in a way you probably never loved my mom and that's okay, too."

Zeke breathed a sigh of relief. "You know there will be an adjustment once we move in together. I've got land and plan to build a house big enough for all of us, and while I don't know if we'll have any more kids, we'll probably be heavily involved in the foster-adopt program we're working on with the orphanage."

"I'm okay with it and will do whatever it takes, Dad. I love those little girls and if you two have more kids, that will be fine too. More to watch over and protect."

"Then it's settled. We're grilling out in a few hours but I'm taking her up to the waterfall shortly to ask her."

Thad smiled. This was turning into the best vacation ever!

***

"Got a minute, Cherub?"

"For you? Always," she said, smiling at the man who had come up behind her and wrapped his arms around her waist, kissing her neck.

"Want to take you for a ride and show you something."

"Okay. Are we going now?"

"Yeah, kids are sorted and we'll be back before we start grilling."

"Then what are we waiting for? Let's ride."

He smiled as he led her to his bike. Checking to be sure her helmet was on, he started the bike and they headed out. He loved the way she fit against him and was glad he had never had another woman on his bike.

***

"Beautiful. Absolutely stunning," she said, looking at the quiet cove with an expression of wonder.

"The water's warm, Cherub, you want to go in?" he asked her as he stripped down.

"Here? Now?"

"Yeah, it's on our land so it's private, Cherub. No one except the wildlife and I will see your gorgeous body."

She blushed because he obviously was blind where she was concerned. She had a typical hourglass shape-big breasts, tiny waist, and hips with thicker thighs than she wanted. Seeing him standing there, naked and aroused, had her stripping off her clothes and walking toward him. Reaching up, she pulled him down for a kiss and moaned when his hands began roaming along her back. "C'mon Cherub," he said, grabbing her hand and leading her into the small pool of water.

As they played and frolicked around the waterfall, she saw another side of him. Now that she was his old lady, it was almost as if another layer had been added to their relationship. He was even more openly affectionate and finally, after playing in the water, he took her behind the waterfall, where there was a ledge. Propping her up on the ledge, he took her hand and looking at her, said, "Cherub, I want to spend the rest of my life with you. I love you beyond measure and know that God brought you and I together in a way that couldn't have come from man. Will you marry me? I know you wear my cut, but I want it all with you- the wedding, the rings, the piece of paper that binds us together until death do we part."

She looked at him with tear-filled eyes and softly said, "Yes. Yes, I will marry you and become your wife. I love you to the bottom of my soul. You make me happier than I've ever been and I look forward to growing old by your side."

He leaned in to kiss her, slipping a ring on her finger that she didn't even know he had. Looking at it, she was stunned to see it had been crafted in such a way that it looked like an infinity circle all the way around, a never-ending love, and he had put all of the kids' birthstones around the diamond that sat in the middle, along with theirs. As the kiss grew more fevered, she leaned into him and wrapped her legs around his waist, putting his hard cock at just the right level. Looking at him, she raised her eyebrows and smirked, saying, "Never knew I would want to make love under a waterfall, handsome, but here we are and we're both ready to go, yeah?"

Looking at her, he nodded as he thrust into her in one smooth move, causing her to moan. "Ah, Cherub, you feel like home," he told her as he set a fast pace. "I don't think this will ever get old, yeah?"

"Less talking, more moving," she said, moaning at the feelings coursing through her body. Reaching down, she palmed one of her breasts and played with the nipple, which had him leaning in and taking the other one in his mouth. Talking ceased other than the moans coming from them both. The angle was perfect, hitting a place she didn't realize was there, and as she climbed higher, she clung to him.

Reaching down, he found her clit and as he kissed her, his tongue mimicking what he was doing with his cock, she felt herself shatter around him. "Zeke!" she cried out even as she held on tighter. One thrust. Two thrusts. Three thrusts and he was coming as well, calling out her name.

They cleaned up in the pool behind the waterfall and played some more in the water, teasing each other in a way that she knew there would be more later that night. Finally climbing out, he went to his bike and grabbed a towel, drying her off then himself so they could get dressed. Reaching for her hand, he led her back to his bike and they repeated their earlier process before he started the bike and they headed back to the cabin.

***

Arriving back at the cabin, Zeke saw that his Brothers had just started the grills, so he had timed it right all the way around. As he helped Angelina off his bike, her ring glinted in the sunlight and he smiled. "Like my ring on your finger, Cherub. Can't wait to add the wedding band to it."

Smiling up at him, she stroked her thumb along his cheek as she reached up for a kiss. "Guess we should figure that one out, huh?"

"Yeah. We can talk later. Right now, I have to get on the grill."

"Going to go check on the girls and spend some time with them," she said as they crossed into the backyard. He headed toward the deck where several grills were heating and she went down to where the kids were playing. Once again, Cailyn was kind of off to the side observing more than playing and she made a mental note to see about getting her checked because something wasn't right.

"Hey girl, did you enjoy your ride?" Eva asked as she came up on the group of old ladies.

"I did, yeah," she said, smiling.

Catching the glint of the ring on her finger, Eva jumped up hollering as she made a mad dash over to her friend. "Oh my gosh! He asked you and you obviously said yes!"

"He did and I did, yes ma'am."

Eva cast a knowing look at her and without words, recognized the look of a woman who had been well-sated. "Mmhmm, looks like you celebrated too," Eva said, teasingly.

Angelina just gave her a smirk and then started giggling as she nodded. "Maybe so."

"Maybe so my hind end," Eva said, careful of the language since a few of the younger kids had started picking up words inappropriate for their age. "So, have you talked about dates or anything?"

Angelina rolled her eyes-for heaven's sake, they had just gotten engaged! "No, we're probably going to talk later. Hey, have you noticed anything about Cailyn? I'm kind of concerned because whenever we're around everyone, she kind of hangs back and doesn't participate. She's always been quieter than Mellie, but it's gotten worse."

Marta spoke up, saying, "She's like that at daycare as well. If there are only a few kids, she's in the thick of things, but when all of them are there, she tends to stay off to the side and just observe, almost as if it's too much or something."

Sighing, Angelina looked at her friends and said, "Guess I'm going to have to get her checked just to ease my mind."

"You know we'll be praying, girl, and anything you need, we'll be there to help," Eva said, coming alongside to give her a hug. "Now, let me see that ring!"

Within minutes, all the old ladies were gathered around as they discussed weddings and showers and everything bridal. Having never been married before, Angelina had no clue what she wanted or didn't want, but figured she and Zeke could work out the details. They chattered as they watched the kids play until Zeke hollered for them to come up and eat.

The blessing said, she got busy fixing the plates for the girls and once they were squared away, she was surprised to find that Zeke had made her plate. "Thanks handsome," she said, bending down to kiss him.

"Mmm, Cherub, kind of like that kind of appreciation," he told her.

She leaned close to his ear and said, "There's more of a different kind for you later."

***

Dinner done, the mess all cleaned up, they sat around talking. Before long, Zeke got up and went inside and came out with a stack of envelopes. Standing up, he looked at his Brothers seated around and said, "Y'all know that we had a problem with our accountant and monies were embezzled. What you may not know is how much was taken or that Angelina has the qualifications to do a forensics search on computers and not only did she trace how much was taken, she also found it. The checks in these envelopes represent what was stolen from you, Brothers. Hopefully, they'll help you live your lives the way you want to." He waited for the cheers and hollers to die down as the Brothers took their envelopes before he said, "Cherub? Can you come up here?"

She gave him a look but got up and stood by his side. "Now, y'all know that Angelina is now my old lady, yeah?" At the murmurs of assent, he continued, "Today, she said yes when I asked her to marry me." More cheers came from the group and he paused again. Looking directly at her, he held out an envelope and at the puzzled look on her face, said, "Cherub, the rest of the Officers and I met and decided that you deserved a portion of what was recovered as well. Because without your help, *none* of the monies would have been recovered. We took it to the Brothers and they agreed as well."

"But…I mean…are you sure? I didn't do it with any kind of expectation, Zeke, other than to help y'all recoup what was taken."

"Yeah, Cherub, we're sure. Use it for whatever your heart desires."

She took the proffered envelope and sat back down and then, upon seeing the amount of the check looked back at him and shook her head in disbelief. "Yes, Cherub."

When a whiny Melora came up rubbing her eyes, she excused herself from the group and gathered up both girls, taking them in and getting them bathed and put down for the night. "Guess what, my sweet girls," she said as she tucked them in.

"What, Momma?" Melora asked.

"Well, Momma is getting married. Mr. Zeke asked me to marry him today and I said yes," she told the two little girls.

"What does married mean?" Cailyn asked.

"It means that Mr. Zeke will be my husband and I'll be his wife. All of us will live together, and he will be your stepfather, like I will be Thad's stepmother."

"Do you get to wear a pretty dress?" Melora questioned.

She laughed softly before replying, "All three of us will wear pretty dresses, sweetie, yeah?"

"Yes, Momma."

"Love you my sweet girls. Sleep tight."

With "love you Mommas" ringing in her ears, she left the room keeping the door cracked and headed to find Zeke. Seeing that everyone else had split for the night with the other parents apparently getting their kids down as well, she headed to his room. He was sitting over in the small seating area that she had somehow missed earlier. "C'mere, Cherub and let's talk, yeah?"

Walking over to him, she sat down and he immediately pulled her into his arms so she was cradled against his chest. "Love you, Cherub."

"Love you, too, Zeke. What...what did you want to talk about?"

"Our pasts, sweetheart. You okay with that?"

She took in a deep breath before replying, "Yeah, I guess so. What do you want to know?"

He looked at her and could see the worry in her eyes. Smoothing back her hair, he kissed the tip of her nose and said, "Nothing bad, sweetheart. I know that Laser was the only one you've been with and based on some comments you've made, as well as your reaction, I'm guessing that you weren't first on his mind whenever you two were physically intimate."

Lowering her eyes because, well *jeez how embarrassing could it be*, she softly said, "No, I wasn't and I was too stupid to realize any different. I know you know he cheated, and would often say I was cold which was why he cheated, but honestly, if he had done a third of the things you've done since knowing me, it would have been a hundred percent better."

Her statement stunned him. "Are you saying you never enjoyed it? At all?"

"Every once in a blue moon, yes, but most of the time, it was over before it started for me."

He tilted her face up so she had to look at him before telling her, "That will *never* be us, Cherub. While I'm sorry my former Brother was an asshole like that to you, I gotta say I'm looking forward to all the ways we're going to improve your education, yeah?"

With her face now flushed from the implication his words left, she gave him a shy smile. "I'm looking forward to it, Zeke. Because today has been wonderful."

Kissing her quickly, he said, "Yeah, Cherub, it has been and I'm kind of looking forward to more of the same tonight. Now, about me. Gayla wasn't my first, and after she left, I only sought out release whenever it was necessary but I mostly took matters into my own hands. But you need to hear me loud and clear, Cherub, okay? *You are my last. Period.* And if there's anything we need to get through or work through, we do it together, no matter what aspect of our lives that involves, from the kitchen to the bedroom, yeah?"

With his words ringing in her ears, she could do nothing but look at him. He was holding her like a beloved, precious thing and he had absolutely no clue how it helped heal broken pieces inside of her that she didn't even know were broken. "I hear you, Zeke. You'll teach me what you like, right?"

"Cherub, *we* will learn together what we like from one another."

"Okay. Can we start on those lessons any time soon?" she asked, smiling up at him.

He grinned back as he replied, "Yeah, Cherub. We can."

Chapter Seventeen

Waking up the next morning cocooned in his arms, she was deliciously sore in a way she had never felt before. Thinking over the past night and how many times they had made love before finally passing out, she wasn't sure if her legs would work yet or not. A nuzzle at her neck and a raspy voice in her ear asking, "Did you sleep okay, Cherub?" had her rolling over and smiling at the man who had made dreams come true without even realizing.

"Yeah, I did, Zeke, although I think I passed out. Oh! I told the girls last night that you asked me to marry you and I said yes."

He looked at her with interest. "What did they say?"

"They wanted to know if they got to wear pretty dresses."

He barked out a surprised laugh before he said, "They can wear whatever they want, Cherub. Do you know when you want to get married?"

"Was hoping you had some ideas?"

"Always been partial to wintertime, Cherub. Would that give you enough time to get things going?"

"Zeke, we don't have to go through a lot of trouble. We can just go to the courthouse."

He looked at her while slowly shaking his head no. "Cherub, you deserve the whole thing: the dress, the shoes, the flowers, all of it and I won't let you settle for anything less, y'hear?"

She closed her eyes in defeat because she knew that President tone meant he was serious. "Okay, Zeke. So, when in the winter?"

"How about the Friday after Thanksgiving, Cherub? Then we'll all be together for Christmas under one roof because I'm presuming that despite the change in our physical relationship, we aren't moving in together until we're married."

"I…I'd rather not, Zeke, more for the kids' sakes than ours. How can we teach one thing and do another? Even us being intimate sort of bugs me for that reason alone and the only thing keeping me from going on the full guilt trip is the fact that we're adults, not children, y'know?"

He looked at her and understanding crossed his face. She had grown up in a rigid household where her morals were always called into question, even though she *was* a good girl. Some things were harder to overcome than others. Cupping her cheek, he kissed her gently before saying, "I get it, Cherub. We can work around it, yeah?"

"Yeah."

"Now, about those lessons…"

Chapter Eighteen

Two Months

She woke up sick to her stomach and was glad that Zeke was out on a run so he wouldn't catch it. Neither would the girls as Dex and Renda had taken them for a week before they started four-year-old PreK. Getting up, she went into the kitchen and got some ginger ale and something for the headache and then went back to bed. Two hours later, she woke up feeling worse with the nausea causing her to fly to the bathroom where she threw up everything including the kitchen sink. A little more ginger ale, which didn't stay down long, and she realized she was hot. She made her way to the kitchen and took her temperature, not surprised to see she was running a fever. Grabbing more ginger ale, she added a bottle of Gatorade and a bottle of water, as well as a pack of saltines, before she headed back to bed. The best thing to do was let it run its course and she once again thanked God that none of the people she loved were home so that they could be spared.

***

Her phone pinging alerted her to an incoming text and she roused enough to see it was from Zeke telling her he would be back the next day and was looking forward to their week together, since Thad was off at a cross country camp before he started back to school the following week. She managed to send him a response saying "okay" before she fell into a restless sleep, broken by occasional bouts of vomiting, as well as shivers even as she knew she was burning up. She sipped at the fluids she had gotten; glad she had grabbed the biggest bottles because she wasn't sure she could make it back to the kitchen to save her life.

***

He pulled up into her driveway the next morning, glad to be back home. He didn't mind the occasional runs, but hated to be away from her or the kids any longer than necessary. He had run by the new house and was excited at the progress made and decided that they would be making a run over there once he had shown her how much he missed her. Knocking on the front door, his smile of greeting turned to concern when she answered the door-her eyes were sunken in and she looked almost green.

"Cherub?" he asked gently.

"Zeke, I've got a bug of some sort…you probably shouldn't…oh no…" she got out before she turned and made her way into the bathroom where she once again started throwing up. *God, how can there be anything left? I've been throwing up for what seems like forever!* She smiled in gratefulness when she felt the cool damp rag against the back of her neck. *Talk about seeing someone at their worst* she thought.

"Cherub? Sweetheart, you're burning up. Where's the thermometer?"

"Bedroom. Nightstand."

He ran and grabbed it and made her take her temperature. Looking her over again and seeing what the result was-one hundred and three-he scooped her up and carried her to his truck, which he had left there in case she needed it when he went on the run. He got her buckled in with a bag "just in case" and then headed to the emergency room. Something was going on beside a simple stomach bug and he wasn't going to rest until he found out what it was.

***

She was triaged quickly and an IV inserted to start her on fluids while they ran tests on her blood and urine. In between bouts of vomiting, she all but collapsed in the bed, and even with the warm blankets they had brought her, she still shivered.

"So, young lady, I see you're having a bit of tummy troubles, eh?" the doctor said as he walked into the room, her chart in his hand.

"Thinking it's more than that, doc," Zeke growled out. "She's running a fever and has chills even though she's burning up."

"Well, she definitely has the flu, so we're starting her on the anti-nausea medicine to stop the throwing up. But there's something else going on. Were you aware you were pregnant?"

She looked over at Zeke in wide-eyed amazement. That had never crossed her mind, after all she had been told the likelihood of ever getting pregnant after the girls was slim to none. The surprise on his face morphed into joy as he smiled at her, and the relief she felt that he wasn't upset was so overwhelming that she burst into tears.

"Ah, Cherub, those better be happy tears, yeah? This is great news!" he said as he tried to console her.

"I-I-I know," she said, sobbing. "It's…it's another miracle, Zeke."

He smiled because it was indeed a miracle. The doctor cleared his throat and said, "Because you've got the flu, Miss Jones, we want to keep you for a day or so to get your fluids straightened out. You were dehydrated. I'll be sending down an ultrasound technician as well so we can make sure everything is okay with the baby."

She nodded, still unable to speak coherently. *A baby…she was having Zeke's baby!*

Shortly after the doctor left, the ultrasound technician came in with the staff obstetrician. As they put the gel on her stomach, she clasped his hand tightly. "Alright you two, ready to hear your baby?" the technician asked as she turned the machine on.

"Yes, please," Zeke said.

Whoosh-whoosh-whoosh…the sound filled the room, strong and fast. The tech tried to point out the various parts, but the two of them were so focused on the miraculous sound they were hearing, they missed much of what she said. She printed off the pictures and handed them to the couple, smiling at the looks of awe she saw on their faces. But her heart turned over when she saw him take the cloth and gently clean off her abdomen before he kissed it gently. She left the couple alone, lost in their own thoughts.

***

As he watched her sleep, he prayed-for their new baby, for her to get better, for the three kids they already had. He had sent a text to Dex in case they had tried to reach her, and to Preacher who had taken Eva over to clean her house before they came up to the hospital. They hadn't stayed long, just long enough for Eva to assure herself that Angelina was going to be okay, and chastise her for not calling.

He reached over and tucked a strand of hair behind her ear, grateful again that God had brought her to him. Seeing her move restlessly, he put his hand on her shoulder and said, "Shhh, Cherub, sleep, yeah? Need you to get better so our baby grows big and strong."

***

What a difference a few days made she thought as she waited for the nurse to bring the discharge papers in so Zeke could take her home. *Home*. After finding out about her pregnancy, they had talked and decided that he and Thad would move into her place until their house was finished. Since she was considered a high-risk pregnancy according to the obstetrician, the build would continue but they wouldn't move into the new house until after the baby was born. And it was a good thing she worked from home because she was on a light bedrest regimen. She could still work from bed and relax and keep everyone happy; the doctor, her friends, and most especially, Zeke.

Seeing the door open, she smiled as he walked into the room, clean clothes in a bag for her. He came over and gave her a kiss and asked, "What can I do to help you get out of here faster?"

"Need a shower, handsome."

He grinned as he helped her get up and over to the bathroom, where he insisted she leave the door cracked in case she needed help. He took the discharge paperwork from the nurse when she finally came in, and as soon as Angelina heard the other voice, he was amazed at how quickly she finished up. "Eager to leave, are you?"

"Uh, yeah. This bed is not my temperpedic that's for sure!" she said, laughing.

Smiling, he sat her in the wheelchair that was hospital policy and then wheeled her out to his waiting truck. Getting her up and settled into the seat, he kissed her and said, "Let's go home, Cherub, yeah?"

"Yeah. Thank you, Zeke."

"For what, Cherub?"

"Not leaving my side other than when I made you go get my clothes today."

"Wild horses couldn't have dragged me away," he told her as he carefully navigated out of the hospital.

Chapter Nineteen

Two Months

It had been a bit of an adjustment moving in together as things had to be shifted so that Thad had his own room. The teen had taken it all in stride, despite her concerns. He loved playing with the two little girls and they adored the attention that he and his friends lavished on them. Plus, living together and being pregnant had her all over the place emotionally, and she found herself crying more than she thought was possible. Zeke had held her to the semi-bedrest and she wasn't allowed to do some of the simplest things, like clean or cook. While most women would exult at that, she knew it was one of her languages of love and how she showed those she loved that she cared. Frustration ate at her and of course, the girls had picked up on it. Then again, she mused, Thad had stepped up there as well, helping the girls keep their room clean, keeping his own room clean which was a miracle for a teen boy, and keeping the yard mowed and trimmed.

Everything came to a head one Saturday morning when she went to get something from her office and he told her he would get it. "Zeke, for heaven's sake, I'm *pregnant* not incapacitated. And I'm doing well, you heard the doctor yourself at the last appointment! I'm not taking any risks or anything, hell, we haven't had sex since we found out!"

He counted to ten. Then he did it again. Finally, feeling calm enough, he said, "Cherub, look, I understand you're frustrated. But you and that baby mean everything and I don't want you doing anything that could bring harm to either of you."

"Zeke, handsome, listen, we are taking care. And, we can still have sex. I promise, nothing will harm the baby. I was only so sick because of the flu, yeah?"

Looking at her, he could see the earnestness in her expression. He knew she wouldn't lie to him about something so important, so he did the only thing he could think of-he kissed her. A quick, close-mouthed kiss that soon turned into a raging inferno of passion that built up to dizzying heights. Scooping her up, he carried her back to their room, closing and locking the door before he carried her over to the bed. "Cherub, you're going to be the death of me," he said, as her hands were everywhere.

"What a way to go, eh, handsome?" she said, teasing him as she worked to pull his shirt off and get his pants down.

He burst into laughter and then took pity on her, stripping the rest of his clothes off before undressing her. Looking at the fullness of her body, already curvy and now even lusher, his eyes darkened and he leaned down to nuzzle at her overly-sensitive breasts while his hand stroked her hip and baby bump.

Hot kisses. Slow kisses. Wicked kisses. He was driving her mad, she thought, as his head descended between her legs, where she was already wet and waiting. "Cherub, hard-pressed to deny you when you're so wet for me," he whispered as his tongue lazily stroked around everywhere but where she wanted it, causing her to writhe and moan. "Ah, Cherub, did you want this?" he asked, as his tongue swiped through her folds to flick against her clit. Her moans egged him on and as he flung her legs over his shoulders, he added two fingers to the mix. It wasn't long before her moans became louder as she came, squeezing his fingers in her hot, silky warmth. He continued his motions until she started to squirm and then moved up her body to draw her in for a deep kiss before he flopped on his back.

"Uh, Zeke? You okay?" she questioned, rolling onto her side.

"I will be, Cherub," he responded as he scooped her so she was straddling him. While she was shy about this position, he loved watching her hair flying around her body and seeing her breasts sway. And when she came? The expression on her face always sent him over as well. "You're going to ride tonight, Cherub," he told her as she knelt and positioned him at her opening. Feeling her sink down onto his hot hard length had him hissing in appreciation. He kept his hands on her hips, allowing her to direct the pace and when she started her climb again, he used his hands to help her grind down to get the pressure she needed. Leaning up slightly, he grabbed a nipple in his mouth and began sucking and the sensations caused her to orgasm, throwing back her head as she undulated and moved on him. With a shout, he emptied himself in her and then caught her as she collapsed onto his chest, both breathing hard. A quick kiss to her forehead and he said, "Love you, Cherub, gets better every time if that's possible."

"I love you too, Zeke. Was that make-up sex?"

He couldn't help it, he started chuckling and then started laughing. "Cherub, if that was your idea of an argument, then I know how well-suited we are because I really try not to argue, yeah? But I need you as much as you need me and I think that as long as we're careful, we'll be just fine."

"Mmm, I agree, handsome. Could have had something to do with my mood, too. I was getting kind of cranky."

"I noticed, Cherub, and understood. We all are just trying to make things easier for you right now with all that you have going on is all."

"Zeke, I am working from home. In bed, at that. You take the girls and pick them up. Thad has been helping by keeping the girls' and his room clean and mowing the yard. Eva or Marta or one of the other old ladies has been bringing food, or you've been cooking or picking up take-out. What on earth do I need made easier?"

"We may have gone a bit overboard."

"A bit? I'd say so, yes. You know the doctor wouldn't steer us wrong and I love how you take care of me, but I cannot go through four more months of this!"

"We'll figure it out, Cherub, yeah?"

She sighed. It was the only concession she was going to get so she decided to change subjects. "Um, you still able to go with me in the morning to take Cailyn?"

"Yeah, Cherub. Definitely have noticed something going on and now she has the weird tics showing up as well."

"I'm doing what I can not to be worried, Zeke, I really am, because I know it does no good to worry."

"Shhh, Cherub. Let me pray for our girl, yeah?" he whispered, drawing her close. At her nod of assent, he began praying aloud, not just for Cailyn, but also for their child.

***

The next day at the pediatrician's office, Angelina detailed all the little things she had noticed going on with Cailyn, but asserted that she had never acted sick or run a fever. The doctor did a full physical, as well as a blood work-up. It was when he dropped something and Cailyn barely flinched that he got an inkling of what might be going on. Telling them to wait one second, he went to another room and came back with another instrument and at their questioning looks, he said, "Needed something stronger. I think, and this is just a guess, that she has lost some of her hearing due to an untreated ear infection."

"But…but she's not had one," Angelina said, a perplexed look on her face.

"Sometimes, kids have little to no symptoms. I'm going to get you over to the ENT in the practice to see if what I suspect is the case or not. Hang on, I want her in today, if possible."

They waited while the doctor went to place a call to his colleague and when he came back in twenty minutes later with a smile on his face, they knew he had accomplished getting them in to see him. "You're all set, go up to the fifth floor, they're waiting for you in the auditory lab, he wants to do a hearing test first before he sees you, okay?"

Thanking him, they took the little girl up to the fifth floor then had to sit out in the waiting room while the technician took her into a room and did the hearing tests that the specialist wanted done. Thirty minutes after that, they were waiting in an exam room when the ENT doctor walked in. "Hello, I'm Dr. Colt, you must be Cailyn?" he asked the little girl. At her nod, he said, "And who are these two grown-ups with you, Cailyn?"

"Momma and Papa Zeke."

"Okay, well, I'm going to talk to them for a few minutes and explain what we did and the results," he told the little girl. "Why don't you go with Nurse Gina to our playroom?"

At a nod from her mother, Cailyn jumped down and went to the nurse who led her out of the room.

"Here's what I found," the doctor started. "She has underdeveloped sinus cavities and that has caused fluid to back up into her ears. Also, the ENT noted that she has unusually large tonsils and adenoids. The combination of the two is giving her what we both believe is a temporary hearing loss."

Angelina looked at Zeke before saying, "What can we do to fix this for her?"

"I'd like to take her tonsils and adenoids out, as well as put tubes in her ears. That should release the fluid and open her ears. Once she's healed, we'll do another hearing test and we will also continue to monitor. We can't make the sinus cavities bigger, but we do have the ability to ensure that her ears stay 'open' so that she can hear the world around her."

"How...how soon?" Angelina asked, mind already working to switch things around.

"I'd like to do it tomorrow if possible."

"To-tomorrow?"

"Yes. Nothing against you or your parenting skills, but she's in that formative phase where she'll start slipping back if she can't hear, and I don't want that for her," the doctor said.

Zeke put his arm around Angelina, saying, "That's fine, doctor. Do you admit the night before or what?"

And with that, he took over, handling all the minor details. They would go home and pack her bag and bring her up later that evening after dinner. Angelina would be allowed to stay with her in her room. Zeke would watch Melora overnight and Eva would come in the morning so Zeke could get to the hospital. "Let's go tell our girl, Cherub," he finally said, seeing the dazed look on her face.

"What are we going to tell her?"

"That the doctor figured out why she can't hear so well and tomorrow morning, she'll take a nap while he fixes it, yeah? We'll keep it simple," he told her, giving her a quick kiss.

***

Once they were through with the doctor, they went and got Cailyn and on the way home, Angelina explained what the doctor wanted to do. Her heart broke when her daughter asked, "Momma, will I be able to hear better?" She had never known she couldn't hear well, and now looking back, she could see all the signs; her standing off away from other kids, not engaging with anyone much except Melora.

"Yes, my sweet girl, the doctor thinks this will help you hear better," she finally said, choking back tears. "Zeke will stay with Mellie and I'll be staying with you, okay?"

"Okay, Momma."

They got home and she went and packed a bag for herself and Cailyn. While in her room, she felt arms go around her waist as a voice whispered in her ear, "Gonna miss having you beside me tonight, Cherub."

Turning, she smiled up at him as she pulled his head down for a kiss. "I'll miss you too, handsome."

"Thinking we might have time for a quickie, yeah?" he said, pulling her close so she could feel him against her belly.

Pulling away, she went down the hall to the girls' room and saw they were playing. "You girls stay in your room for a bit, yeah? Momma needs to get cleaned up before we head back with Cailyn."

Melora looked at her and said, "Okay, Momma. Can we watch a movie?"

"Yes, baby, whatever you want, just stay in here, okay?"

The two little girls went to their TV and picked out a movie from the rack and handed it to her. She got them set up and then went back to her room where she closed and locked the door. Walking over to where he was sitting on the end of the bed, she said, "Now, what were you saying about a quickie?"

Grinning, he pulled her down so she straddled him, then scooted them back on the bed. Her sundress made access easy and he all but ripped her panties off while she pulled the dress over her head. When all that remained was her bra and his jeans, he rolled her off him so he could remove his jeans and boxers and rolling back, he saw she had taken off her bra. He took a moment to absorb how she looked, belly burgeoning with his child, breasts enlarged, and her glorious hair all around her. With a low growl, he practically pounced on her, pulling her close as he began kissing her.

Knowing they had little time but wanting to make it good for her, he reached between them and was shocked at how wet for him she was. "Cherub, you're soaked," he whispered as he nuzzled behind her ear.

"Mmhm," she moaned as she ran her hands along his side and down to fondle his cock. "Natural reaction for me whenever you're near and naked. The pregnancy hormones help, too," she said, giggling.

He kept them on their sides but lifted her leg over his hip so he could slide right in. She moaned in pleasure, it seemed that this angle had him hitting another spot that she liked. As he set a rapid pace, she found herself clinging to him and when he leaned down and captured a nipple in his mouth, she came hard, milking his cock with everything she had. He rolled them without breaking a connection, bringing both her legs around his waist and he continued his thrusts, causing her to climb again. Reaching between them, he gathered a bit of the wetness and stroked across her clit-once, twice, three times-before she shattered beneath him once again. The sensation of her hot, tight pussy clenching caused him to come and he did so with a roar before claiming her mouth in a bruising kiss.

***

One quick shower later, and they were both dressed again and ready to head back up to the hospital with Cailyn. Before leaving their room, he gathered her in his arms and said, "Love you Cherub. Love you and the girls more than I can say."

She smiled up at him and kissed him lightly, saying, "Never thought I'd fall in love again, Zeke. I love you so very much it scares me sometimes. You get there when you can, I know you've got club stuff to take care of first thing."

"Preacher's already on it and Eva is coming to get Melora tonight. They'll bring Thad up in the morning, but tonight? I'm going to be there with you two, yeah?"

"It's mighty cozy in those cots, Zeke," she said, giggling.

"Cherub, don't care if you have to lay on top of me, you won't go through this alone, yeah?"

"Mmkay. Thank you, Zeke."

"For?"

"Being the man you are - loyal, caring, generous. You treat me and the girls like we are cherished beings, loved beyond words."

"That's because you are all cherished and loved beyond words, Cherub," he said softly as he leaned down and kissed her. "Now, c'mon, we've got a girl who has a date with a doctor."

***

Back at the hospital, they got Cailyn checked in and even though she was scared, when the nurses brought in a small hospital gown and mask for her doll, she was ecstatic. Her room was a private room and Angelina was happy to see that the "cot" actually pulled out into a full-sized bed. When she remarked on it, the nurse said, "We had so many parents wanting to stay that the decision was made to remodel and renovate so that they could both stay. Hard enough on a child who is undergoing surgery to have to decide whether they want mommy or daddy with them, so we made it easy."

"Well, I love it, because I'm not leaving her and he's not leaving us, so…"

The nurse laughed, saying, "Yeah, I get it."

The most challenging part was when they had to insert the IV. The little girl fought until Zeke came over and cradled her in his arms, crooning to her and telling her what a big girl she was for letting them get her ready for the doctor to make her better. Angelina stood there with one hand over her baby bump, which was more than a bump for some reason, and tears in her eyes at how gently he dealt with the little girl. Within a matter of minutes, the IV was secured and she was settled in her bed once again. He handed her the remote and said, "Since you have the bed with all the gadgets, you get the remote. Want to find a movie, Princess?"

She grinned shyly as she shook her head yes. He helped her turn the television on and was pleasantly surprised that there was a kids movie button. Once again, the nurse spoke up, saying, "Since this is the pediatric wing, we had them change a few things to make it kid-friendly. One of those things, aside from the sleeping arrangements, was the selection they had on television to watch. All the channels are kid oriented. You won't find any CNN or ESPN in here."

Cailyn found a movie she wanted to watch and settled in, her baby at her side. Angelina got "ready" for bed, slipping into some yoga pants and an overlarge T-shirt while Zeke swapped his jeans for lounge pants. They dimmed the lights except for the one over Cailyn's bed and before she fell asleep completely, held hands with her while Zeke prayed for the upcoming surgery and a quick recovery.

***

The next morning dawned bright and sunny and they both dressed quickly, not knowing what time they would take her down for her surgery. Hearing a knock at the door, they saw Preacher and Eva walk in with Thad carrying Melora, who was clutching her baby in her hands. "She wanted to see her," Eva said in greeting. "She was getting upset, so we figured it was best to just bring her up here." The adults watched as Melora climbed into the bed with her sister so they were snuggled together.

As they waited, Angelina prayed silently. She asked for forgiveness for not noticing. She gave thanks for a positive outcome.

Another knock at the door had the adults pausing their conversation. This time, it was the doctor, already dressed for the surgery. "Well, well, well, what do we have here? *Two* Cailyns?" he asked the two little girls, who were now giggling. "Hmm, so I have to guess which one I'm going to operate on today?"

More giggles from the girls. "Let's see-Cailyn has strawberry-blonde...oh, no, that won't work, will it? You both have the same hair color. Cailyn is the...no, you both look alike! I know, I bet the little girl I'm going to operate on today has a hospital gown on, a band on her arm and a tube in her hand!"

At that, Melora pointed to Cailyn, saying, "It's her, doctor, I'm her sister."

He smiled at both girls then asked, "Are you going to help Cailyn eat popsicles after her surgery?"

Wide-eyed at the mention of the "magic word", Melora merely nodded.

"Well, let's get this show on the road then, okay?" the doctor asked as a gurney was brought in by two nurses. "Mom, dad, we have a waiting room for you to stay in that's near recovery. Either myself or a nurse will be out when it's finished up to let you know how it goes, okay?"

Angelina nodded and stood, going over to her daughter who looked so very small on the gurney. "Love you my sweet girl. You'll be just fine, yeah?" she asked as she bent down and kissed her. "Momma will see you soon."

Kisses from everyone else done with, Zeke held hands with them all as he prayed for the surgery before they wheeled the little girl out, still clutching her baby in her hands. As they passed the surgery waiting room, the nurse pointed it out and they headed in there, four adults and one little girl who was already missing her twin.

Thad was busy keeping Melora entertained while Zeke and Preacher talked about some upcoming events they were planning, including the foster parent training. Eva had gone down to grab drinks for everyone and Angelina was sitting there, trying to figure out a crochet pattern, when she heard "MOMMA!" in a terror-soaked tone coming from somewhere down the hall. Dropping everything, she ran toward the sound and found her daughter, sitting up in bed grabbing her throat and sobbing. "Shhh, shhh, Caycoo, Momma's right here. Stop screaming baby, you'll hurt your throat, okay?" Once Cailyn calmed, she crawled up into the bed with her, careful of the IV, and cradled her while the recovery room nurse checked vitals.

"It's not usual protocol for you to be in bed with her, however, if it will keep her calm, I don't much mind," the nurse said as she brought over a cup of ice chips.

"Protocol or not, if she needs me, I'm here," Angelina said. "Why does she seem so hyper-sensitive?" she asked the nurse, while looking down at the tear-stained face of her little girl who was slowly sucking on the ice chips. Pain still filled her little eyes and it broke her heart. "Can she have some pain meds?"

"Everyone reacts to anesthesia differently. Once it's out of her system, she'll be fine," the nurse said. "Let me get some pain meds into her IV, it's important to stay ahead of the pain. We've also got a special necklace for you to wear, Cailyn, and we'll give it to you once we get back up to your room, okay?" At the little girl's nod, she said, "We're going to take y'all up to her room now and I guess, mom, you're going for the ride as well."

Angelina looked down and saw how Cailyn had curled herself around her and started chuckling. "I guess I am. Should I do the princess wave or something as we pass people?"

The nurse, keeping a straight face, said, "Absolutely!"

***

The first night was hell on earth. They bumped up her fluids to try to help flush the anesthesia out faster, but that meant she kept soaking the pull-ups. Rather than call the nurse each time, Angelina would get up, get her cleaned up and a fresh one put on. When she stumbled and almost fell after the fourth trip to change Cailyn, Zeke spoke up, saying, "Cherub, I've got this. You come and sleep, yeah?"

"Are you...I mean..." she stammered out, so tired she couldn't think straight.

"Sweetheart, you're falling asleep on your feet. Come sleep, I've got this, okay?"

She finally nodded and he helped her back into bed. As he leaned over to kiss her, he realized she was already asleep. Covering her up fully, he kissed the top of her head, whispering, "I've got you, Cherub." Then he went and sat in the chair next to the little girl, ready to take care of whatever she needed through the rest of the night.

***

One Week

Angelina woke with a start, realizing that she hadn't heard Cailyn through the monitor. Rolling over, she saw that the bed beside her was empty, so she carefully got up and out of the bed and moved as quickly as possible down to the girls' bedroom. Looking in the room, she saw it was empty so she headed down the hall and into the kitchen, where she found both girls sitting in their highchairs with Zeke at the stove, making pancakes and Thad gathering the plates and silverware to set the table. "Morning, y'all, what do we have here?" she asked.

"Morning, Cherub," he said, pulling her closer for a kiss. "Heard the girls and decided to let you try and sleep a bit longer. They wanted pancakes so here we are, waiting for the griddle to heat up."

She grinned and went over to the girls, giving them both kisses before saying, "How are you feeling this morning, sweet girl?" as she looked at Cailyn.

"No hurt, Momma," the little girl said as she pointed to her throat.

"Do you think you can handle pancakes?"

"Yes, Momma. No hurt."

She looked over at Zeke and he nodded. Thinking about it, she finally stated, "Well, they're soft enough so we'll cut them up really small, okay? And I'm so happy that you seem to be hearing better too!"

Cailyn grinned. She didn't really understand, all she knew was that what sounded a lot like buzzing before and indistinct words had become clearer after she went to the place where she had to take a nap for the doctor. Her throat had hurt for a few days, but her Momma made sure she took special medicine and it went away. And her Papa Zeke had been there too, helping Momma take care of her, but she was glad to be home with Mellie.

Chapter Twenty

Two Months

Zeke let out a steady breath as he looked over the reports he had gotten from Angelina. Each of the businesses was doing better than the year before, and she had been investing the extra monies in various money market accounts until he told her where he wanted them invested. He smiled thinking about her -she was "bigger than a house," according to her, but he loved how she looked carrying their baby. They had chosen not to know the sex, which had driven her girls crazy because they wanted to shop, but as Angelina said, since it was a miracle baby, she was content with either a boy or a girl so long as it was healthy. At a little more than seven months, she glowed with health and vitality and he grinned thinking of all the creative ways they had come up with to make love. Things were, out of necessity, a bit slower than they liked but he loved watching her face as they made that climb together. She was so expressive in her responses and he thanked God, again, for bringing her into his life.

***

"Eva, there's no way we're going to find a dress to fit me!" Angelina said. "I know the wedding is just around the corner, but seriously? I look like a baby whale!"

"And I happen to know a man who is partial to you, Shamu!" her friend said, laughing.

Rolling her eyes, she worked to get up waving off both Eva and Marta and their help. "Fine. Let's go see if Omar the tentmaker has anything in off-white for a bride-to-be."

They took their time shopping, not wanting to wear her out, but eventually, they ended up at a little shop that had recently opened. Walking in, they heard, "I'll be right out!" from somewhere in the back of the store and they browsed while waiting for the clerk. Hearing a noise, they turned and saw a tiny slip of a woman coming toward them, a big smile on her face as she said, "How can I help you ladies today?"

"Um, well, I'm looking for something to wear for my wedding," Angelina finally said. "I'm not sure you'll have anything since I'm bigger than Mt. Everest."

Eva started laughing. Each time Angel spoke up, she made herself bigger than she truly was and had now compared herself to a whale and a mountain. "Ignore her. She's full of pregnancy hormones. She's getting married the day after Thanksgiving and we want something pretty that will, uh, expand if needed since we have about a month to go."

The clerk said, "Well, my name is Rose and I'm the owner here and I think I might have something for you to try on. We can order it in the right color, as well as the next size if you think you need it, or I can order the size you're wearing now as well as the bigger size, just in case." With that statement, she went toward the back of the store, the other three women following her. Stopping at a display, she looked back at Angelina, squinted in thought, then went back to the rack and pulled out two different maxi dresses. "What do you think, ladies?" she asked.

Marta reached for one and Eva the other, leaving Angelina to stand there. "I like this one, it looks like it's going to flow well," Eva said as she put it against Angelina. "The neck isn't too low; I know you don't like hanging out everywhere."

Angelina looked down at the dress Eva had pressed against her. It would come up under her breasts, but flow out from there. She wasn't ashamed of her baby bump, not by a long shot, but wanted pretty pictures. "Let me try both on, yeah? We can make a better decision then, I think," she said, taking the other dress that Marta held and looked at Rose. "Where are the dressing rooms?"

Rose led her to the dressing rooms and said, "Just come on out when you get the first one on, okay?"

She smiled at the clerk and said, "I'll be out in a few!"

Roughly five minutes later, she emerged from the dressing room to gasps. "Is that good or bad?" she asked her friends.

Eva pulled out her phone and snapped a quick picture before turning it around so Angelina could see. "Oh Angel, he would love this one!"

She looked at the picture and was stunned. Yes, you could tell she was pregnant, but the way the dress flowed around her, it wasn't horribly obvious. Shades of her past, she supposed, that she felt a bit guilty being pregnant, again, "out of wedlock," but whatever.

Marta, after walking all around her, said, "I love it, but let's try the other one on too, yeah?"

"I agree," Rose said.

Angelina went back into the dressing room and changed dresses. She could tell from the looks on the three women's faces that they didn't like this one as well. Eva snapped another picture and showed it to her and looking objectively, she had to agree. It was pretty but it didn't flow as well as the other one. "I kind of like the first one better, what do y'all think?" she finally asked.

All three women looked at each other before saying, almost at the same time, "We like the first one better too!"

"Then it's settled. Now we have to find dresses for the girls and y'all."

Rose led them to another display after asking about her colors. "I have no clue. These two are handling 'everything' since I'm on bedrest," Angelina told her. "But we're getting married the day after Thanksgiving if that helps any?"

Eva laughed, saying, "We went with cream and a mossy green."

With that, Rose's eyes lit up and she started pulling dresses from the rack. "These would complement perfectly, don't you ladies think?"

Looking at what she had pulled out, both Eva and Marta agreed and they got their sizes and headed off to the dressing rooms to try them on. "Now, what sizes are your girls?"

"They just turned four so a four or five will work, they're a bit small for their age."

"Twins? How delightful!"

Angelina smiled as she pulled out her phone and went to her photos. She looked through several before she found one with both the girls standing there, grinning up at her and then turned it so Rose could see.

"Oh my goodness! They're beautiful, just like their momma!"

"Thank you. I think they are too, but am a bit biased," Angelina said. "Do you have anything in their size?"

"Hmm, let me go look in the back. I just got in a shipment of kids dresses so I might. I'll be right back," she said, already headed to the back of the store.

"Angel? What do you think?" Eva said as both she and Marta came out of the dressing rooms.

"Oh wow. They look good, don't you think? Will they work with what y'all have planned for the colors?"

"Yeah, hon, they'll work," Marta said.

"Then I think we have *our* dresses. Rose went to the back to see if she had anything that would work for the girls. She said she just got a new shipment in with kids dresses."

As they waited, they browsed the rest of the store and before she knew it, she had a handful of comfortable looking flowy tops that would be perfect during this last month and a half of the pregnancy. It seemed like time was flying by so fast, but she knew it was only because she was excited to be getting married.

"What has that look on your face, Angel?" Marta asked, coming up alongside her and taking the clothes out of her arms.

"Thinking about Zeke."

"Aha, you're so busted!" Eva said, bursting into laughter.

"Y'all have no idea, none at all. Laser was good to me, in his own way, but he could be a jerk too. I loved him as much as I knew what love was, of course, but honestly? I had absolutely *no clue* what that word meant until Zeke Morgan came into my life. He is the epitome of that chapter about love in scripture. I know that things will grow and change as we do, but the foundation? It's there."

"You're right, we don't know how Laser was, only what you've shared. But we do know Zeke and he is what you say – kind and selfless and loving, but firm when he needs to be."

"Well, let's grab these things and go get something to eat and I'll educate you a bit, yeah?" Angelina said.

They gathered their items and headed to the checkout line where Rose was waiting. She showed them the dresses she had gotten in for little girls and they picked out one that would best work with the chosen colors. She took all of the items and began ringing them up only when

Angelina presented her card, Rose shook her head no, saying, "The gentleman called and gave his information over the phone."

"Gentleman?" Angelina asked.

"Yes, said his name was Zeke Morgan."

Eva and Marta started laughing. "He's taking care of you, Angel, so you might as well get used to it," Eva finally said once she calmed down.

***

Over lunch, she told her two friends a little about what life with Laser had been like. When they started making noise to tell her how sorry they were, she stopped them, saying, "He was far better than what I grew up in, trust me. And, he loved me to the best of *his* ability, even if it wasn't always great. With Zeke in my life, I now know the difference, but until he came along? I thought it was the norm, so no feeling bad or sorry for me. God has given me more than I ever expected or anticipated and I am beyond blessed, yeah?"

Eva sat back and looked at her and could see the peace radiating from her. "Okay. I think I get it, Angel, and we'll leave him where he needs to be, in the past."

Angelina nodded. "You two ready? I should probably get back to the house before he sends out a search party. He's still going over the top a bit, but I understand."

"He wants to make sure you're okay and taking care of you and the baby," Marta said as she gathered their lunch trash to throw away. "One of y'all grab me a refill while I toss this, yeah? And Angel? You might want to hit the restroom so we don't have to stop every twenty minutes."

Laughing, Angelina got out of the booth and made her way into the ladies room. Taking care of business, she was washing her hands when she heard her phone chime. Looking at the text, she laughed out loud, it was a picture of the girls who had managed to talk the teenagers into playing with them, apparently.

As the three women headed back out and got into the car, Eva asked, "Are y'all ready for our last trip to the mountains for the season?"

A dreamy look came over Angelina's face-she had loved each trip they took to the cabins, but the first one would always hold a special place in her heart. "Yeah, we're ready. I'm surprised Zeke let me bake. Oh wait, he didn't, not really. He brought everything to the table, let me mix it and put it together, then he and Thad manned the oven and shit," she told the other two women.

***

Later that afternoon, the girls down for their naps, she curled up on the couch to watch a sappy Lifetime movie. She was surprised at how long she had lasted shopping, but thinking about it, she realized that they hadn't gone to too many places, and they had taken plenty of breaks in between each stop. Her mind went to the last shop-Rose had a well-stocked inventory and she decided that she would be buying more items from her once she was no longer pregnant.

He came in and realized the house was unusually quiet. He knew Thad was at a lock-in at church, so that explained the "no teens running through the house" that had become his normal. Checking the girls' room, he saw they were still asleep so he closed their door again and headed into the family room where he heard the television softly playing. Rounding the end of the couch, he saw her, curled up on her side, feet tucked behind her, and sound asleep. He pulled down the throw that was across the back of the couch and gently covered her before placing a soft kiss on her head, then he went into their room to change into something to lounge around the house in as they weren't leaving until the morning for the cabin. Returning to the family room, he eased in behind her and pulled her close, wrapping his arm over their baby. When she went to roll, he moved to his back and maneuvered her so her back was against the back of the couch and she lay draped across him. "Zeke?" she asked, sleep making her voice husky.

"Yeah, Cherub. Didn't mean to wake you, go back to sleep. Just wanted to cuddle with my girl."

"Mmkay. Love you."

"I love you, Cherub," he quietly said, kissing her forehead. "Now, rest, yeah? You had a busy morning and afternoon, and I have plans for us tonight." She smiled sleepily because she knew what his plans were and she was totally onboard with them.

***

He woke up to little girl giggles and a foot stuck in his ribs. Opening his eyes, he saw Cailyn and Melora standing there watching him. He looked down and could see the baby kicking him. Hearing a low chuckle on his chest, he glanced over to the side and saw Angelina smiling at him. "I see our baby got you, yeah?" she asked as she placed her hand on her stomach where the tiny foot was protruding.

"Yeah, seems that way, Cherub," he replied, giving her a quick kiss before he moved to sit up. "What has you two little princesses giggling?"

"You were taking a nap, Papa Zeke," Cailyn said. He grinned at her and mussed her hair. Ever since her surgery, she had been more outgoing and her speech was even sounding clearer.

"Yes, I was, sweetie. Everyone else was taking a nap, so I figured I would join in."

Angelina held up her hand for help off the couch. "What did you want for dinner, Zeke?"

"Figured we would go out tonight, Cherub. No sense in cooking when I can take my three best girls out for dinner. Did you get all the packing done?"

"I did, yes. Figured we would load up in the morning?"

"Yeah, Cherub. Thad and I will take care of it when we get up tomorrow. He's coming home early from the lock-in for the run. Now, c'mon, ladies. Who is ready to eat?"

She grinned at him before she headed off to get ready to go out. "Girls, go ahead and go potty, okay?" she asked as she went into their room. Walking over to the closet, she grabbed an outfit and headed into the bathroom for a quick shower. The heat and humidity, unusual for this time of year, combined with her expanding belly, had her feeling like she needed two and three showers a day.

"Cherub?"

"In here, Zeke," she called out from the bathroom, having gotten out of the shower and now trying to dry off.

He walked into the bathroom and stopped to stare. She had piled her hair up on her head to keep it as dry as possible and her skin glowed from her recent shower. Stepping over to her, he took the towel and bent down to dry her legs and feet, eliciting a smile. As he placed a kiss on her stomach, the baby kicked and she burst into laughter at the expression on his face. "C'mon, Cherub, we have some hungry kids," he told her as he helped her with her panties and capris.

"Zeke, I can dress myself you know," she told him.

"I know but it's more fun if I help," he replied.

"How so? All you manage to do is get me all worked up!"

He smirked at her as he dropped a kiss on her collarbone where her pulse beat. "Mmhmm. Just think about later, Cherub," he said as he pulled her close for a kiss.

Several minutes later, he let her go and gave her a pat, saying, "Now, c'mon, Cherub."

She finished getting ready and they grabbed the girls and headed out for dinner.

***

Later, back at home and getting ready for bed, he waited for her to join him. As she came out from the bathroom, his stomach tightened-she had no clue how beautiful she looked with her hair falling around her shoulders and her lush, pregnant body glowing with life. "C'mere, Cherub," he said, patting the bed next to him. She crawled into bed and he spent a few minutes getting her situated the way he wanted her, which had her giggling. "What's so funny?" he asked as he kissed her.

"You realize you do that all the time, right?" she asked, answering his question with a question. "You arrange me how you want me every single time!"

He saw the humor in her statement because he did, in fact, do that when they were in bed together. He loved her touching him and loved being able to touch her and caress her. "Mmhmm, I want you touching me whenever possible."

"I see," she said, a half smile gracing her lips.

"What's that smile for?"

"You'll see," she told him as she began softly stroking him. Scooting down the bed, she curled up on his thigh, her attention now diverted as she grabbed him. A soft hiss of air escaped him as she leaned forward and took him into her mouth, her hand stroking where her mouth couldn't reach. Not to be outdone, he rearranged her so that he was free to warm her up, his mouth and fingers soon causing her to moan around him. "Zeke," she breathed out.

He maneuvered her again so she was straddling him and pulled her face down so he could kiss her, long and deep. Feeling her wet heat, he leaned back and said, "Ride me, Cherub." She needed no invitation and he soon felt her sliding down along his length. Low groans from them both had him gripping her hips before he began moving her up and down in the movement they both enjoyed. She leaned forward, using her knees to help her keep the momentum and he reached a hand up and fondled her breast before leaning his mouth closer and taking a nipple into his mouth. Words now impossible, only the sounds of their moans and the slapping of flesh filled the air. As he felt his orgasm approaching, he reached between the two of them and added some pressure against her clit with his thumb.

"Oh my God, Zeke," she cried out, her body clenching as she threw her head back and her hips continued to move and jerk. Seeing the visual of her lost in the throes of her own orgasm caused him to follow close behind and he called out her name as he found his own release.

Spent, she collapsed on him, both breathing hard. "Gets better every time, Cherub," he whispered in her ear before he kissed her forehead. "Let me get you cleaned up so we can get some sleep, yeah?"

She was nearly asleep when he spooned behind her, pulling her close. "I love you, Zeke," she mumbled.

"Love you too, Cherub. Sleep well."

Chapter Twenty-one

Thanksgiving Week

She was getting married in three days. *Three days*. Dex and Renda were up, as were a lot of the Brothers and their old ladies from South Georgia. Her girls were busy baking and getting things ready for Thanksgiving, as well as the wedding. She had finally "won" and while everyone was upset, since it *was* her day, she had them going to the Justice of the Peace on Wednesday morning so that they could enjoy Thanksgiving and then they were holding a combination reception/baby shower on Friday at the clubhouse. The biggest difference between the original plans and now was that everyone was going with them to the courthouse for the ceremony. She and Zeke would stay in town and then come out to the clubhouse the next day for Thanksgiving dinner.

"Cherub?"

"In here, Zeke," she called out from the closet.

"What are you doing, sweetheart?"

"Trying to find shoes that fit now that my feet seem to have grown," she replied.

"Cherub, we can get married with you barefoot if you need to be," he told her.

"No, I think I have a pair of ballet flats down here somewhere."

He looked at her – she was bigger than before and still had about a month to go. "Here, let me, sweetheart," he said, helping her back out to sit on the bed. "What color are they?"

"Hmmm, I don't remember exactly, maybe light pink? No, cream?"

He unearthed a pair of what he thought she was thinking and she pounced on them, saying, "Yes, these are them."

"Let me help you with them, Cherub," he said, as he knelt in front of her. He carefully slipped first one and then the other on. "Do they feel okay?"

She wiggled her toes experimentally. "They kind of feel tight, Zeke. Now what am I going to do?"

He removed them and got the Crocs she had been wearing back on her feet before he helped her up. "Looks like we're going to find you something to wear, Cherub. Renda has the girls, that's what I was coming to tell you, so that we can run some errands."

"What would I do without you?"

"God willing, you'll never have to find out, sweetheart."

***

New shoes purchased and crisis averted, they spent the afternoon running errands before they went to the new house. It was pretty much done and he had been slowly moving things over so that after they were married, they could move in fully. As they pulled up in front of the house, she gasped. He had been busy! The Christmas lights were already on the house and there were a few inflatables that he had placed around the yard. "Oh Zeke, when did you find the time?"

"I didn't, not exactly. Had Thad and the prospects help with this," he told her as he carefully got her out of his truck. There had been a light snow so he was keeping his hand at her back as he walked her up the stairs and onto the porch. Unlocking the door, he opened it and brought her inside, stealing a kiss under the mistletoe that was already hanging in the foyer. "Wanted to show you something," he said, leading her through the living area and into the kitchen before they went down into the basement.

She looked around in amazement. The last time she had been over, they had talked about what they wanted to do with the full basement and she had given a few suggestions but told him that ultimately, it would be up to him. He showed her the three guest rooms that were down there now, along with a kitchenette area that had a refrigerator and microwave so any guests wouldn't have to come all the way upstairs for drinks. He had even put in a coffee bar and a game room with a huge television. "Zeke, this is amazing," she finally said.

"Figured when Dex and Renda or Debbie and Pongo came up, you'd want them here instead of the clubhouse," he replied.

"It's perfect. And I suspect Renda's going to want to be here when the baby finally arrives."

He chuckled because she had already made that clear to Dex, who had shared it with him.

Another reason to make sure this part of the house was finished. "Come and see what I've done with the girls' room," he told her as he led her back upstairs.

The house itself was a sprawling quasi-ranch with an upstairs that held all the bedrooms including a nursery that was directly off the master, and five more bedrooms. He led her to one of the doors and opened it and she walked into a castle. The only things missing were the twin canopy beds but he had said the prospects would be moving everything else over in the next few days. "They're going to love it, Zeke."

Taking her hand, he led her to their room. Since he loved the colors at her current house, he had replicated them in their bedroom. The only difference was he had gotten a bigger bed for them, envisioning times where they would curl up with the girls to watch movies. Wide eyes glanced up at him as she took in the room. He leaned down and captured her lips with his, teasing a sigh from her as she melted into his arms. Long minutes passed before he pulled away, feathering kisses along her jaw before he placed one last kiss on her forehead. "Love you, Cherub. 'til my last breath."

"Til my last breath, Zeke," she whispered.

***

Wednesday dawned bright and clear, a fresh snowfall the night before making everything all pristine and fresh. She rolled over to find the spot next to her empty and she smiled. *I'm going to the chapel and I'm gonna get married* she thought before she started giggling. Easing out of bed, she went in search of some sustenance before she got ready. In the kitchen, she stopped and stared. The girls were in their highchairs, Dex and Zeke sitting at the kitchen table with cups of coffee, and Renda moving around making breakfast, ordering Thad around like he was her sous chef. "What's going on?" she asked.

"We're going to eat breakfast and then get ready to head to the courthouse," Renda told her as she plated some eggs for the girls. "Now, c'mon and sit down, bride-to-be, and get some breakfast. Going to be a busy day."

Breakfast was a fun-filled affair and once it was finished and everything cleaned up, Renda pushed her toward the bedroom saying, "Go get beautiful, gorgeous."

"Cherub?"

She turned around to find him directly behind her. "Hmm?"

"Need any help?"

Blushing, she smiled at him and said, "Nuh-uh, handsome, you gotta wait for this," as she moved her hands down her body. He just grinned as he leaned in for a quick kiss.

***

An hour later, everyone all dressed and ready to go, he led her and the girls out to his truck. Thad was riding with Dex and Renda and they would take the girls after they were done at the courthouse.

"Momma?" Cailyn asked.

"Yeah, sweetie?"

"Today is when Papa Zeke becomes our daddy?"

Tears came unbidden to her eyes before she said, "Yeah, sweetie."

"We can call him Daddy?"

"You can call him Daddy or Papa Zeke, whichever you want, okay?"

"I'm going to call him Daddy," Cailyn stated.

"Me too," Melora said.

Zeke took in a deep breath, as this was far more than he had ever expected. Looking at the two little girls, all dressed up to watch their mom get married, he said, "I'm proud to be your Daddy, girls."

***

Once at the courthouse, things seemed to move fast. Before she knew it, they were in the judge's chambers. Looking at the group, the judge cleared his throat and then called out to his secretary, "Mabel, can you check for me and see if we can go down into the garden?"

Looking at the couple, he said, "We have a garden that is pretty well-protected against the elements. Thinking it would be a better place for this given the fact that two little girls are all dressed up to watch their momma get married."

A few moments later, the secretary came into the room and said, "It's free, Judge. Y'all follow me, okay?"

Down in the garden, which was decorated with Christmas lights and poinsettias, the judge got them arranged and then, before he began the ceremony, said, "Is there anything either of you want to say?"

Taking a deep breath, Angelina looked up at Zeke and softly said, "I was lost and you found me and restored me and redeemed me to be the woman that God wants me to be. Much as Ruth did for Boaz, I promise that where you go, I will go and where you stay, I will stay. I will love you 'til my last breath."

Zeke, smiling down at her, lifted his hand and softly stroked her cheek before he said, "In the broadest sense of the word, I am your kinsman-redeemer, Cherub. Where you are is home and as long as you are by my side, we can weather any and every storm as long as we cling to the third cord that binds us."

With tears shimmering in her eyes, she softly smiled. The judge, witnessing the obvious love the couple had, cleared his throat from the lump that had formed before saying, "While I normally don't do this, I can tell that this occasion calls for it," before he quoted 1 Corinthians 13, ending with, "Do you have rings to exchange?"

Within minutes, the ceremony was finished and she heard the judge say, "You may now kiss your bride."

Strong arms enveloped her with one hand coming up to cup her face in a way that had her swooning. Leaning in, he said, "I love you, Cherub, til my last breath," before he captured her lips in a soft but meaningful kiss that held a promise for all their tomorrows.

As they pulled apart, four little arms embraced them and they heard, "Momma, Daddy!" Letting her go, he crouched down to hug both little girls to him, unaware that Renda had been snapping pictures the whole time. He kissed both girls on their foreheads, eliciting giggles, before he stood and found his son waiting for a hug. Angelina, standing there as witness to the pure love the three kids were showing, found herself sniffling through her smile.

Renda got their attention and asked for a family picture, which the secretary, Mabel, gladly took. Leaving the courthouse, paperwork in hand, the kids went with Renda and Dex and Zeke took her hand and led her to his truck. Carefully helping her in, he helped her buckle before turning her head and kissing her. "Hello, Mrs. Morgan," he whispered.

"Hi, Mr. Morgan," she said, softly.

He took her to one of the nicest hotels in the area and once they were changed out of their wedding finery, he looked at her and said, "What do you want to do, Cherub? Thought we could get something to eat and then see what comes up."

She gave him a mischievous look and a wink before she stepped into his arms and looped hers around his neck. "I thought," she said, giving him a quick kiss, "that we could start out over there," and she motioned to the bed, "and see what comes up."

He grinned and scooped her up in his arms, carrying her over to the bed despite her protests that she was too heavy. He didn't care if she weighted one hundred pounds or five hundred, he just wanted her and he set out to show her just how loved and cherished she truly was, grateful that room service was available.

***

Thanksgiving Day

Arriving at the clubhouse, they came in the door to whoops and hollers and cheers which caused Angelina to blush and Zeke to smile even more than he already was. Two small streaks came running toward them and he bent, catching the two little girls up in his arms. "Give your Momma a kiss, girls," he said as he leaned closer to his bride. *His bride* he thought. The previous afternoon and evening had been spent in bed, making love and napping. He had gotten up briefly to order room service but other than that, they had stayed holed up in their room together. And he wouldn't change a thing.

Angelina leaned up to give him a quick kiss, saying, "I'm going to go help get the meal out, handsome."

"Okay, Cherub."

He got the girls settled and chatted with Preacher and Dex and several other Brothers while the women brought the food to the table. Once everything was in place, he stood and blessed the meal before he began the task of passing plates. Thankfully, the old ladies had carved the turkey and ham, so it was a matter of getting what he wanted and passing it on down the line. When he realized that Angelina was taking items for the girls' plates and not her own, he nodded at Renda who got another plate and quickly filled it for her. Once the girls had their plates, he reached over and squeezed Angelina's hand and when she looked at him questioningly, he leaned over and said, "I'm sorry, Cherub. I wasn't thinking."

"About what, Zeke?"

"It didn't dawn on me that you were working on their plates or I would have taken one of the girls' plates so you didn't have to wait to eat," he told her.

"No worries, handsome. There's plenty enough to go around, yeah?"

Conversation around the table was free-flowing and laughter filled the air. Zeke smiled, since

Angelina had come so many things had turned around for their chapter, and he gave thanks again that she had come to them. He knew they complemented each other and couldn't wait to see what the future held for them.

"Zeke, are you paying attention?"

"Hmm?" he asked, realizing that Preacher had been speaking to him.

"I said, these crazy women have just hatched a plan to go Black Friday shopping! The teens will watch the kids and we have to go to 'carry bags' or some such nonsense. Can't you put your foot down?"

"Handsome, we figured if we went out later once the stores reopened, we could be done by breakfast and come back and sleep for a bit before the kids all got up," Angelina said. "You know it's going to get harder for me to shop next month."

"Cherub, don't want you wearing yourself out," he said.

"I won't. We've got a plan and as soon as the kids all go to bed, we're going to make lists and divide and conquer."

"What do you mean?" he asked cautiously.

"Well, if we figure out what we want from the different stores, we can all leave together and then split off and tackle the various stores. We'll figure the money out when we get back."

He thought about what she had said and decided it sounded good. "I like that idea, Cherub. May become a new tradition for us, yeah?"

She smiled at him and leaned over to kiss him. "I've got a few more I want to start with you, Mr. Morgan," she whispered in his ear.

"I see," he said, nuzzling her jawline.

The feasting over, the kids sat with the teens who helped them compose their wish lists, Cailyn and Melora sitting in Thad's lap while Amelia wrote down what they said. Zeke drew Angelina aside and said, "Cherub, what say you and I tackle the toy store? And what do you think about the bigger gifts coming from us instead of Santa?"

She thought about it for a minute and then said, "I like that idea, Zeke, because not every 'Santa' has as much money to spend. What can we do for the kids at the orphanage?"

He looked at her and then said, "I nearly forgot with everything else going on, Cherub. Since we got the classes done, the families who participated will be taking in their foster kids in the next few weeks. I think all the children except the special needs babies who still need medical care will be in a home for Christmas."

As tears streamed down her face, he pulled her close to comfort her. "It's okay, Cherub."

"I-I-I didn't realize it would have such an impact," she cried. "Let's find out what they can use for the babies so we can take care of that, yeah?"

Her generosity knew no bounds he thought. "We can do that, Cherub. The Brothers and I have been collecting money to help defray the cost."

"We could always use the money from my check," she said.

"Cherub, thinking you're going to need a bigger vehicle, yeah?"

"Zeke, my SUV is paid for and has a good book value. I'm sure we can get a good trade-in on it and pay the rest with my check and *still* have money to help."

Thad, coming in during the conversation, piped up and said, "My buddy, Jonas, just got put in that place last week. He was living with his grandma and she died and he has nobody else."

"Jonas? Jonas Blackburn?"

"Yeah, Dad."

"Cherub, do you trust me?"

"With my life, Zeke, why?"

"Jonas is a year younger than Thad, good kid with a shitty life. His grandparents were raising him when his folks both died of an overdose. Think we have room for another teenage boy?"

She looked at the young man who was now her stepson. Then, she looked at the man who was her husband. Her giggles started out quiet and then ramped up until she was doubled over laughing.

"Cherub? What's so funny?"

"You-you-you…you want to *willingly* feed another teenage boy," she stammered out between her giggles. "It's a good thing we have a huge refrigerator and walk-in freezer, as well as a giant pantry."

Seeing the humor in what she said, he began chuckling as well. "Thad? Let me make some calls and see if we can fix that for Jonas, yeah?"

Thad grinned at his dad and Angel before saying, "Thanks, Dad. I won't say anything until you know for sure, okay?"

"That would be wise because sometimes, things don't move very fast."

***

The kids now down for the night, the Brothers and their old ladies made their master lists from the wishlists they had written and then divided them up. With Zeke, Angelina, Dex, Renda, Preacher and Eva in three vehicles, and the others split up into their vehicles, they headed off to the main shopping area where most of the stores were located. The plan was for each group to get as much on their list as possible from their assigned stores, then they would go over to Zeke and Angelina's new house and divvy it up. Anything that was left would be bought online.

Hours later, with bags and boxes "everywhere", they arrived at the house and began the arduous task of dividing up the purchases. Angelina made copies of the kids' wishlists and the receipts, promising that she would let each couple know if they owed the buying couple any more money. She suspected, however, that Zeke and Dex were going to take care of the difference because that was how they tended to be.

Once they had hidden what was bought for the girls and Thad, as well as Jonas, because she had a good feeling about it and had texted Thad while they were out asking what he liked, they all went to the diner for breakfast.

"Thinking I like this tradition, Cherub," Zeke said as the waitress poured coffee and juice for the group. "We had a lot of fun and managed to get everything the kids wanted."

Angelina looked at Eva and Marta and Sass and then said, "Now we just have to wrap it all, right girls?"

Good-natured groans and laughter rang out. "We can send the girls out for paper and tape and stuff later," Eva said. "I know that Tally and Amelia wanted to hit some of the sales themselves."

"Works for me," Angelina replied. "We've got time."

***

Arriving back at the clubhouse, he could see how tired Angelina was, so he went and found Tally and asked her if she would babysit for the girls for a few hours before she went shopping. "Yes, sir. It'll give me a little more money to shop with too!"

He chuckled at the teen's response. She loved the girls and was good with them and he didn't mind paying her to keep them if it meant his bride could rest. Speaking of…he looked around and spotted her curled up in a chair. At first glance, she looked like she was just sitting there, but as he got closer, he saw she had fallen asleep. Brushing back the hair that had fallen in her face, he scooped her up and gently carried her to his room where he got her settled before he curled up with her. It had been a busy twenty-four hours and he needed a nap as well!

Chapter Twenty-two

Later that day, refreshed from her nap as well as a bit of lovemaking from her husband, she walked out of his room at the clubhouse and was amazed at the room's transformation. The old ladies now had the main room decorated for the reception and baby shower, and even had two different cake and gift tables set up.

"Y'all are absolutely amazing," she said to Eva.

"We love y'all and want to show you just how much," she replied.

"Okay so what are we doing first?"

"We figured the baby shower first, then some dinner, then the reception. We catered in the dinner for the reception, of course," Marta said, coming into the room.

"Okay, and are the guys part of the baby shower?"

"This one is, Cherub," Zeke said as he walked up behind her and pulled her back into his chest.

She let her girls lead her over to the place of honor, Zeke sitting next to her, and was moved to tears at the beautiful devotional that Renda did for the baby. As Marta, Sass, Debbie, Eva and Renda served up cake and punch, she sat and basked in the absolute joy she was feeling. The girls were miracles but this baby? Was a blessing from God.

"So, did you guys choose names?"

They looked at each other and smiled before Zeke answered saying, "Yeah, we did, but we're not sharing. Angelina doesn't believe in naming a child before they're here because she says the name may not fit the personality."

She caught the looks from her friends and said, "What? Y'all know how I am, I had six names for the girls, remember?"

Renda and Debbie burst out laughing. "Yeah, that's right. Forgot about that, Angel!"

"Eva, do you think the girls can come out and help unwrap?"

"I think that's a great idea, sweetie, let me go get them," she responded. Standing, she made her way to the playroom and within minutes, Melora and Cailyn were sitting in front of their parents, waiting to help open the presents.

***

An hour later, all the gifts opened and the list for thank you cards safely in Zeke's pocket, he turned to her and said, "Cherub, got something for you as well. It's outside, though, so let me get your jacket, yeah?"

She gave him a quizzical look, after all, what could he have gotten her that would be outside? She waited patiently until he came back and helped her up and led her outside, where a Suburban sat there, gleaming in the late afternoon sun. "Zeke? What-what did you do?"

He leaned down and kissed her softly before he said, "You're going to need a bigger vehicle, Cherub, so I got us two of these, and will give Thad my truck. Didn't know what you would want to do with yours so it's at the house."

She just shook her head at him. He saw a problem and fixed it. "Thank you, handsome, it's most generous of you."

"Cherub? Look at me," he asked.

She looked at him and he whispered, "They're paid for, Cherub. We had more than enough to buy them."

What else could she say? "Love you, Zeke. Thank you for taking care of us, all of us, as well as you do."

"'Til my last breath, Cherub. 'Til my last breath."

***

While they had been outside admiring her new vehicle, the prospects had cleared the floor and moved the gifts into Zeke's truck to take them over to the new house. And once again, the clubhouse was transformed, this time it was for their wedding reception. They cut cake and fed each other, ignoring the catcalls to smoosh it into one another's face. She had too much respect for him as a man and as the MC's President to do something like that, and he cherished her too much. Besides, the secret thrill she got when he leaned down and captured her finger in his mouth to lick the frosting off was *totally* worth not smashing cake into his face. The slight blush on her face amused him and he pressed in closer and whispered, "Think we need more of that frosting for later, Cherub. It's quite…delectable."

"Eva? Gonna dance with my bride now," he said.

As the DJ started the music, he held out his hand and simply said, "Dance with me, Cherub."

With the strains of Anne Murray's "Could I Have This Dance?" playing, he led her out to the makeshift dance floor and pulled her into his arms. Her head on his shoulder, she let the words flow through her down to her soul. "Zeke? You couldn't have picked a more perfect song."

"I agree, Cherub. I love you so very much," he said, as he leaned down and began singing along. Lost in each other, they didn't realize that most of the old ladies had tears streaming down their faces. As the song ended, another one came on, Alabama's "There's No Way" and other couples joined them on the floor. When the third song came on, Lonestar's "You're Like Coming Home," she realized just how intertwined they had become. She couldn't imagine life without him in it and pulled his head close to whisper that in his ear. "Feel the same way," he told her as he captured her lips in a sweet, promise-filled kiss.

The DJ broke in after the third song, simply saying, "Congratulations to the newlyweds. Now, from what I understand, dinner is waiting to be served so if y'all could head to the tables and eat, we'll get back to dancing shortly."

Laughter broke out because Zeke had done things the way *he* wanted, not the way that the old ladies had set up. "It's all good, handsome. I needed to feel your arms around me," she told him as they went to the head table, where Eva and Renda already had the girls set up. Unbeknownst to her, they had decided to keep the girls and Thad so she and Zeke could have a few days together by themselves and would be staying at the new house with all the kids.

As the night wore on, the dancing continued and she found herself dancing with Zeke frequently, but also doing a few line dances with "her girls" and then dancing with Dex and Preacher. During their dance, Dex looked down at her glowing face and said, "So happy for you, Angel. I knew God had a bigger plan for your life."

"I finally believe you, Dex," she said. "My cup runneth over, as the saying goes."

Around ten that night, Zeke leaned over and whispered in her ear, "You ready to go, Cherub?"

"But what about the kids?"

"Dex and Renda are staying at the house with the three kids. And when we get back, we'll go pick up Jonas."

"We're going away? I wasn't expecting that, Zeke. I'm…I'm not packed or anything! And we're picking up Jonas? You heard back already?"

"Your girls took care of it for you, but I don't think you'll need too much in the way of clothes. As for Jonas, we can talk about that later, Cherub. Got other things on my mind right now."

Damn, she was beautiful but with that blush stealing across her cheeks? Magnificent he thought.

"Then yes, I'm ready, handsome. Been ready for quite some time now, actually."

He stood and took her hand and at a nod to Dex, the room quieted down. Zeke looked at his family and friends and simply said, "Thank you. We are blessed in so many ways by each and every one of you and I thank God for every one of you in this room. Y'all know the drill, Preacher has the reins but Dex and his VP and their old ladies are here as well while we're gone, so behave yourselves, yeah?"

"Zeke, need to say bye to the girls."

He walked over to where the two little girls were curled up on Dex's lap and picked each of them up so that she could kiss and cuddle them for a few seconds. "Okay sweet girls, y'all listen to Uncle Dex and Aunt Renda, yeah? Behave yourselves and remember your manners. I love you both so very much."

"I love you, Momma," Cailyn said, her little voice sleepy sounding.

"Love you, Momma and Daddy," Melora told them. "We'll be good."

Zeke smiled down at the two little girls before he kissed them and told them he loved them and they would see them in a few days.

***

He had found a smaller cabin further in the mountains for them, fully stocked so they could stay in if they chose, but close enough to a town if they wanted to go out. He suspected a lot of their time would be spent in bed and whether it was sleeping or making love, he didn't care so long as she was in his arms. As he drove, they talked about the past three days, laughing over the "new" Black Friday tradition. Growing serious for a few minutes, they discussed the potential challenges bringing Jonas into their home and he felt his spirit calm when she laid her hand on his arm and softly said, "Whatever we face, as long as we're together, we'll get through, Zeke."

She dozed off about halfway into the trip, leaving him to his thoughts, which centered on her and their children. He knew their beginning hadn't been conventional, but he didn't regret one minute of it. Finally pulling up to the cabin, he saw that there had been a light snowfall, so he shut the Suburban down and went to get her out and carry her in. She woke as he was lifting her, asking, "Zeke? Are we here? I can walk, handsome."

He ignored her comments as he walked up the steps, carefully setting her upright while he unlocked the door. Once he had accomplished that, he picked her up bridal style and carried her across the threshold, saying, "Welcome to your home away from home for the next few days, Mrs. Morgan."

As he set her down, she pulled him close and standing on tiptoe, kissed him. A short, sweet kiss that heated quickly, causing him to pull back and say, "Hold that thought, Cherub, let me get our stuff inside, yeah?"

She nodded and bent to take off her shoes, prompting him to shake his head at her. "That's my pleasure to take care of, Cherub."

"Fine. Do you want something to drink?" she asked as she headed toward the kitchen.

"How about some hot chocolate?"

"Mmm, yeah, that sounds good, handsome. I'll get it made for us, okay?"

He nodded as he headed back out to the Suburban to grab their bags and lock it up. Looking around, he could see they were in for some more snow and when he got back inside, he went ahead and started a fire, grateful that the caretakers had brought firewood into the cabin already. Hearing footsteps, he glanced back to see her coming toward him, two mugs of hot chocolate in her hands. "Here you go, handsome," she said, handing him his mug. Taking a sip, he marveled at how she managed to make it the way he remembered as a kid. They sat in companionable silence, warming up their insides with the tasty drink and when they were finished, he gathered their glasses and returned them to the kitchen before he held his hand out to her.

"C'mon, Cherub, let's go get cleaned up and see what we can get ourselves into, yeah?"

She smirked at him as she let him help her up and then let out a surprised yelp when he scooped her up and carried her into the bathroom. While he lit the candles, she got the water started in the tub and was standing back up when she felt his heat at her back. "You look beautiful, Angelina. Stunningly beautiful," he said as he turned her around. "Let's get you out of this, yeah?"

Words escaped her at the look on his face and there was no way she could adequately describe what that look was doing to her insides. Love, lust, passion and desire were all there on blatant display, making his handsome face even more so. She reached up a hand and stroked it down his cheek and jaw before she said, "I love you, Zeke, and thank God every day for bringing you into my life."

He kissed her nose and then turned her around again to begin working on the buttons down the back of her dress. She knew the minute he saw what was underneath by his sharp intake of breath. She might be pregnant, but she had managed to find a maternity corset that displayed all her assets for her new husband. As the dress slid down her arms and pooled at her feet, he turned her again and placed his hands on her hips. "Ah, Cherub, beautiful." He loosened and removed the corset and she soon found herself standing there, naked. Her lush figure was glowing with the new life growing within and he palmed her stomach as he drew her close for a kiss. She could feel how much he wanted her through his clothes and her hands began working to unbutton his shirt even as she returned his kisses which were growing more fevered. "Let me get it, Cherub," he finally said, pulling back and making quick work of his own clothing. He turned her so they were facing the mirror, her back to his front, and he watched her as his hands roamed from her breasts to her swollen abdomen. Stepping back, he led her to the tub and helped her in, climbing in behind her and pulling her back to rest against his chest. Her giggles had him peering over her shoulder, unsure of why she would be laughing especially with his hard-on pressed against her back. "Cherub? What has you giggling?"

"Look, Zeke! The way I'm laying has my belly looking like a whale and my bellybutton is the blow spout!"

He started chuckling at her fanciful words. "Cherub, you're gorgeous as the mother-to-be of this baby, yeah?"

Tilting her head back, she looked at him before she placed a quick kiss on the underside of his jaw, watching his eyes darken in passion. He took the washcloth and began to thoroughly but quickly bathe her, dropping kisses and nips wherever he could reach. By the time he was done bathing them both, she felt as if she was going to combust. Once he had them out of the tub, he carefully dried her off and then dropped to his knees and after kissing her stomach, spread her legs. "Ah, Cherub, you're so wet already," he said.

"Mmmhmm. Perpetual state of affairs whenever you're around, Zeke," she said, moaning as his tongue reached out to tease between her folds. Without warning, he stood and scooped her back up and carried her into the bedroom where he laid her gently in the center of the bed before he followed her down.

"Now, where was I?" he asked after kissing her thoroughly. "Ah yes, I remember."

She lost herself to his talented touch and tongue. Seconds morphed into minutes and it wasn't long before she was shattering beneath him, crying out his name as she rode out her orgasm, his fingers and tongue still stroking. Placing a final kiss on her abdomen, he made his way back up her body, stopping to suckle each breast which had her on the verge again before he claimed her mouth. "God, Zeke, I need you, please," she moaned out.

"As much as I need you, Cherub," he replied as he slowly entered her. He knew he wouldn't last long, she was still pulsing around him and he was determined she would shatter again before he did. He rolled them gently so she was astride him and he watched as she played with her nipples while she moved. Hands now on her hips, he set a rhythm that would draw it out as long as possible because he loved seeing her expressive face when they made love. When she leaned down to kiss him, he raised up and all thought fled until they were both moving in sync. He felt the fluttering begin and sped up, adding a circular thumb motion to her clit.

"Zeke!" she cried out as she shattered in his arms. He managed three more thrusts before he joined her, reveling in how she gave herself over to him.

As he held her close while they caught their breath, he kissed her forehead, saying, "I love you, my sweet Cherub."

"Love you too, Zeke," she replied, sounding sleepy now that she was sated.

He chuckled lightly and without letting her out of his grasp, pulled the covers up and over them both, saying, "Let's nap for a bit, yeah? Been a busy few days and I need you rested."

"Mmmhmm, sounds good."

Chapter Twenty-three

Once again, he scooped her up and carried her across the threshold, something she had given up telling him he didn't need to do because he enjoyed it so much, and as he set her back down, she looked around in amazement. She knew the prospects were going to move them and Zeke had mentioned they were taking care of that while they were gone, but she figured she would be puttering and putting things away when they got home. To walk in and find it all done? Priceless and yet another reason she loved this crazy family.

"Where are the girls and Thad?" she asked.

"Not here, at least not until I call Dex," he replied. "We've got a little time, Cherub, so let's go christen our new bed, yeah?"

She shook her head at him, but followed along willingly. He was insatiable and she was finding that where he was concerned? So was she.

***

She woke slowly to giggles. Opening her eyes, she saw her sweet girls laying on the bed next to her, a grinning Zeke propped against the headboard. "Hey my sweet girls," she said, her voice raspy.

"Momma!" Cailyn cried, "We missed you!"

"Mmm, I missed you girls as well. Were you good for Uncle Dex and Aunt Renda?"

"Yes. We helped move, Momma," Melora replied.

"You did?" she asked, sitting up.

"We did, Aunt Renda brought our toys over and we put them away!"

"I'm glad you two helped. Do you want to show me?"

The two little girls got off the bed and as she was attempting to, she felt him lean into her for a kiss. "You okay, Cherub? You sound a little hoarse."

She looked at him and noted the smug look on his face. "Hmm, don't know *why* I would be hoarse, handsome."

He chuckled as he got off the bed to help her up. Dropping a kiss on her forehead, he followed the two little girls while she went to the bathroom. Once in the girls' room, she praised them for the good job they did by not only unpacking their things, but keeping them picked up when they weren't playing. "Girls? When Thad gets home, we're going to go pick up Jonas and do some shopping."

"Can we have a snack?"

Laughing, she led them into the kitchen and made them a snack. Sitting at the kitchen table, she started a list of things they would need while out shopping. "Zeke? It's a good thing we've got the Suburban."

He glanced down at her list and started laughing. "Cherub? You want to find a Christmas tree too?"

"Yeah. While I love live trees, I can't exactly get under it to keep it watered, so I want to get a pre-lit one. And we'll need ornaments and stuff too. Maybe we should do shopping for Jonas first and then eat and then go get a tree?"

He opened Google on his phone and typed in pre-lit trees. Finding several at a local store, he asked her which one she liked best and when she decided, he called a prospect to the house and sent him to get the tree. "There, Cherub. Now we can shop for Jonas and ornaments, but I'm still taking us all out to eat tonight, yeah?"

"Yeah, Zeke. That works for me. Do you want to go over the reports and stuff tomorrow?"

"That's soon enough, Cherub. Everything's in good shape and we have a house full of kids to get in order, yeah?"

She laughed. Another dream realized and he was giving it to her once again. A houseful of kids. She was still laughing when Thad came in from school. "Hey Dad, hey Angel. Why are you laughing?"

"Hey yourself. I'm laughing because your dad is fulfilling dreams again."

"What dreams, Cherub?"

Looking at him, she smiled softly and said, "Kids, Zeke. We're going to have a house full of them, something I never dreamed would be possible."

He leaned down and kissed her before whispering, "Love you Cherub and any dream that's within my power to make happen, I'll do it."

Thad rolled his eyes at their display but after a month or so of living under the same roof, he was getting used to it. If they were in a room together, they were touching in some capacity. He was thrilled that his dad was so happy and prayed that what he thought he had with Amelia would stand the test of time. Shaking his head, he said, "So, we going to get Jonas? I know he's stoked."

"Yeah, we were just waiting on you, then we'll go shopping for anything he needs or wants, and then we have Christmas decorations to get."

"Will there be food in there at any point?" the teen asked.

"Yeah. Gonna feed my growing tribe," Zeke replied as he gently cuffed his son.

"Then can we get this show on the road? Oh, and Dad? I think he needs a phone. His grams did the best she could, but he really needs a lot of stuff."

"We'll take care of it, Thad. He's got a home with us as long as he wants one, yeah?"

Thad smiled in relief. While Jonas was a year younger, he had skipped a grade and they had been friends for a long time. His home life was crap until his grandparents stepped in, but they didn't have the resources to ensure a growing kid always had what he needed. Thad remembered years of others trying to bully Jonas until he got bigger.

***

At the orphanage while Zeke and Angelina filled out the paperwork, Thad helped Jonas pack his belongings. "Hey man, I appreciate your folks doing this for me," Jonas said.

"I wish we could have done it a long time ago, but it wouldn't have been right taking you from your grandparents, y'know?"

"Yeah. You've been my best friend for years, Thad. Not sure I would have made it without you helping me."

"It's what friends are for and maybe someday, if we join Heaven's Sinners, we'll be Brothers."

Zeke, walking up on the conversation, smiled inside. He had a sneaking suspicion his Cherub wouldn't rest until they had adopted the teen, so

they'd be brothers in all ways except blood.
"You boys ready?" he asked.

"Yeah, Dad."

"Yes, sir."

"Jonas? Appreciate the manners, especially since we're teaching the girls their manners, but you don't have to be formal, okay?"

"Yes, sir, I mean…okay."

As they walked back out to the car, Jonas was surprised when one of the twins reached up to hold his hand. He looked down at the little girl and she smiled at him, saying, "Now we have *two* bubbas!" At her words, the fear he had that things would be awkward melted and he found himself smiling back.

***

Man, she was a helluva shopper he thought as he watched her telling the boys what she wanted them to look for when they hit the department store. When Jonas looked like he would argue, she got a stubborn look on her face and told him that there would be no arguing, she knew he had stuff he needed and if he didn't go pick it out, she would and her favorite colors were pink and yellow. While the boys were shopping for clothes and stuff for his new room, she and the girls were over in the Christmas section buying ornaments and decorations for the inside of the house. "Cherub? What do you think about this for the fireplace?" he asked, pointing at a manger scene. She went to where he was standing and looked at it carefully, it wasn't gaudy, which she detested, and the pieces were big enough not to be dwarfed on their mantel in the family room.

"I like it," she said softly. "It will be perfect on the mantle, don't you think?"

"Yeah, Cherub. Do we need wrapping paper?"

She started laughing at his question, causing him to quirk his eyebrows at her. "Why are you laughing?"

"Eva and Marta had the girls grab a bunch of paper on Black Friday, handsome, so all we need to get is tape."

He went to the bin that held multi-packs of tape and tossed several in the cart. About that time, the boys came back with two shopping carts full of stuff. One held the bedding Jonas had picked out and the other had clothes and stuff for school. Looking at the four carts they had, all filled to the brim, he smiled. Never in his wildest dreams could he have imagined having a wife again, let along four and a half children!

***

Later that night, Jonas' room all squared away and the kids down for the night, they sat in the family room with a Christmas movie playing softly in the background. When he noticed her feet were swollen, he got her situated and began rubbing her feet. "Cherub, is this normal?" he asked.

"Sometimes. I was on them a lot today, so I'll be mindful tomorrow," she told him.

He continued to rub them until her moans reached his ears. "Cherub? Thinking it's our bedtime now, yeah?"

Seeing the look on his face, she readily agreed.

Chapter Twenty-four

Christmas Eve

The past several weeks had passed in a whirlwind, with parties at the daycare, more shopping, wrapping, and baking and Angelina was glad that it was nearing the end. She still had a few weeks left before the baby was due and movement had become harder without help. Waddling into the kitchen before everyone got up, she started getting stuff together to make breakfast. As she puttered, Christmas music playing softly in the background, she smiled at how much her life had changed. They had spoken at length with one another, as well as Jonas, and they had a special gift for him tomorrow morning. A slight twinge in her low back gave her pause, but she shrugged it off as nothing. She felt his strong arms go around her as he placed a kiss beneath her ear. "Merry Christmas, Cherub."

Turning, she placed her hands on his chest and leaned up for a kiss saying, "Merry Christmas, Zeke."

"What can I do to help?"

"Um, well, the muffins are done, the bacon is almost done, and I'm about to start the French toast," she replied.

"You sit down, I'll take care of it," he told her, leading her to a chair and then raising her legs so they were elevated.

Once he had enough cooked, he went and told the kids to wash up and come eat, then helped her get the girls' plates ready. *Daycare has been so good for them* she thought, listening to them giggle and talk about Santa Claus. The teens said little, waiting on Zeke to say the blessing before they started eating.

While they ate, they discussed the plans for the day. It had been snowing steadily so Zeke asked the boys to take the girls outside and build a snowman, which had the little girls all excited. Dex and Renda were due up later in the day, so he helped her get something started in the crockpot for that night's dinner. The kids now outside, they worked to clean the kitchen in companionable silence. Once done, he led her into the family room where they curled up on the chaise lounge to enjoy the Christmas tree lights and fire he had lit in the fireplace. "Zeke?"

"Hmm, Cherub?"

"Hate we have to wait now, handsome."

"Angelina, look at me," he said in *that voice*. She looked up at him and saw him looking down at her tenderly. "Cherub, I waited a long time for someone like you in my life. A few weeks is nothing. You and the baby are more important to me," he told her as he kissed her softly.

"I know, was just thinking about you and me naked under the tree," she said wistfully.

"Well, there's always next year and if we want *that* to happen, we'll be putting one in our room, yeah?"

Realizing that by next year there would be *five* kids ranging from almost a year old to nearly eighteen, she started giggling. "We are going to become extremely creative, aren't we, Zeke?"

"Absolutely. We may have a lot of lunch meetings during the school day that involve our bedroom," he told her.

They were interrupted by Cailyn coming into the room saying, "Come look, Daddy, Momma! See what we did!"

He helped her up and got a coat on her, then helped her out to the porch where a family of snowmen had been built. The boys had built the bigger ones, but each girl had made a smaller one. "You did a wonderful job!" she praised. "Now, who wants some hot chocolate? Maybe a movie?"

With the girls settled in with a Christmas movie, the boys went down to the game room to play their video games and she and Zeke curled up on the chaise, where she promptly fell asleep.

***

"Sweetie, I don't think you can get any bigger," Renda said, giving Angelina a once-over. "Are y'all sure there's only one baby in there?"

"Yep. The doctor said there's just one but it's a big one."

"Are you feeling okay? You look tired."

"I'm glad you're here. I think the baby is going to come sooner rather than later," she admitted to her friend. "But *not* before Santa creates some magic for two little girls."

That afternoon, the girls "helped" make cookies for Santa, which necessitated a kitchen clean-up. Santa's plate of cookies ready, they spent the rest of the afternoon before dinner building a puzzle. Meanwhile, she tried to hide the occasional twinges she was feeling. *Too soon* she thought. *You're too soon, sweet baby.*

***

Dinner and baths finally done, Zeke read the Christmas Story from the bible before he read "The Night Before Christmas" to the girls. They had talked at length and decided that as long as they gave the girls a good foundation, a little fun was fine. Tucking the girls in was proving challenging as their excitement had them bouncing off the walls. Zeke finally used his president voice which left the girls wide-eyed. He told them that Santa couldn't come until they were asleep and if they weren't sleeping when it was time for him to come to their house, he might have to pass by and possibly wouldn't have time to come back. Within minutes, the two little girls were asleep, their dolls clutched in their arms.

Once the boys headed off to bed, the adults worked to set up the gifts around the Christmas tree. Angelina knew that the dollhouse they had found for the girls for their room was going to be a hit and she couldn't wait to see their faces the next morning. Knowing the girls would be getting up early, they didn't stay up late, opting for as much sleep as possible.

***

She woke the next morning and the occasional twinges had become a dull ache. *God, just let me get through them opening their Christmas presents* she thought. With a little assistance from Zeke, she got up and took care of business and got dressed before heading out to start the coffee and turn the tree on. The girls weren't up yet, so the adults and teens waited in the kitchen until finally, they heard the footsteps coming down the hall. "HE CAME!" Cailyn screamed. "MELLIE! SANTA CAME! HE ATE ALL OUR COOKIES AND DRANK OUR MILK!"

Hearing the excitement in her daughter's voice and how clearly she was speaking, Angelina brushed back tears. As the adults and teens headed into the family room, she made her way over to the chaise while Zeke went over to the tree to start handing out presents. Excitement coursed through her at the girls' reactions. They hadn't gone too overboard on any of the kids, but got them gifts that they knew they wanted and needed. Once the girls were done and playing, the boys started their opening. When Jonas got to his last gift and saw what it contained, he turned tear-filled eyes to Zeke and Angelina. "You...you want to adopt me?"

"Absolutely. You're a part of our family now and we want you to know it," Zeke said.

"I accept, thank you both," Jonas said, as tears ran down his face.

***

Later that morning, after breakfast, she went to lay down, citing the early morning as the reason for her nap. Zeke could tell something wasn't right, so he followed her in and caught her doubled up. "Cherub? How long you been in labor?"

"Um, possibly since last night," she said as she straightened up from her latest contraction.

He hollered for Dex and Renda, who came running at the tone in his voice as he bundled her up and carried her out to the truck. "We're headed to the hospital, looks like Baby Morgan is anxious to come today," he told the couple. "Can you stay with the kids?"

"We'll get them together and be up there shortly, you go and take care of Angel," Dex responded.

***

At the hospital, her doctor was paged while she was admitted. Coming into the room, the doctor grinned and said, "Seems he or she wants to give y'all a special Christmas gift, yeah?"

"It's too soon," Angelina said as another contraction wracked her body.

"Based on the size of the baby, even if you're a few weeks early, we'll be just fine," the doctor said soothingly as she prepared to check how far along Angelina was in her labor. "Hmm, okay, well, folks, looks like you're going to have a Christmas baby," she finally said after sitting back up and disposing of her gloves.

Zeke brushed her hair back from her forehead before he leaned down and kissed it. "It's going to be fine, Cherub, yeah?"

She panted through the next contraction while the nurses got the room ready for the impending birth. "Mmmhmm, handsome. Will you pray?"

Seeing her distress, he put his hands on her stomach and prayed softly. When the fetal monitor that they had inserted started going off, the doctor and nurses went into immediate action and she was wheeled away from him and toward an operating room, leaving him standing there.

***

Thirty minutes later, the door to the waiting room opened and the doctor came in, apologizing to him for their haste. Both Angelina's and the baby's blood pressure had dropped, signifying they were both in distress and she had had no choice but to perform an emergency cesarean. "Would you like to meet your baby?" she asked.

"Yes, and how is my wife?" he asked in response.

"She's awake, because we had the IVs in, we gave her a local instead of general anesthesia. Come with me and I'll take you to her."

He followed the doctor down the hallway, his heart hammering in his chest. He had continued to pray after they took Angelina, not knowing what was going on, just knowing she was in capable hands. Entering the recovery room, he saw her laying there, a bundle all swaddled in her arms. Seeing him, she smiled, her whole face lighting up, as she said, "Want to meet your youngest daughter?"

A girl he thought. *Thank You, God.* Out loud, he asked, "And how are mommy and baby doing?"

"Mommy is higher than a kite thanks to the great medicines she has onboard in her IV, baby girl seems to be just fine as well, weighing in at a whopping nine pounds despite being a few weeks early!"

"And her name, Cherub?"

"What do you think about Merri Noelle Morgan?"

Looking down at the tiny face curled next to his wife's breast, he thought about her suggestion.

"I like it, Cherub. I like it a lot. Welcome to the world, Merri Noelle, I'm your Daddy," he said as he gently picked up and cradled the sleeping baby. "Wait until your big brothers and sisters see you." Sitting carefully on the side of the bed, he cuddled his wife and quietly prayed over them, thanking God for no real complications and asking for a quick recovery.

***

Finally in her room and settled, Zeke went and got the rest of the kids, who were waiting out in the waiting room with Dex and Renda, along with Preacher and Eva and their kids. He was humbled that his Brothers and their families had come out on Christmas Day no less to bear witness to his family's addition. Standing up in front of them, he said, "She's doing well, will be out of commission for a few weeks while the stitches heal, but she and the baby are both fine. Thank you all for coming, it means more than you'll ever know."

"It's what family does, Brother," Preacher called out. "Now, you gonna tell us what the baby's name is?"

"Give me a few, Preach, we want to tell the kids first and I'm going to take them in now, yeah?"

With that, he picked up the twins and walked back down to his wife's room, the teens trailing behind with silly grins on their faces. Opening her door, he saw her sitting up with the baby and carried the girls over to her bedside. Carefully setting them down and with the boys on the other side, he said, "Say hello to your baby sister, Merri Noelle."

Epilogue

Ten Years Later

Thad looked around the reception hall, his eyes falling on his parents as they swayed to the music. He grinned thinking about the past ten years and how much joy was now in *all* their lives, thanks to Angelina. Instead of being an only child, he now had five sisters and three brothers, some through birth and the rest through adoption, but he didn't care one bit. The crazy, chaotic, loving environment he had lived in as a teen and a young adult until he finally went off to college had pointed him in the direction he wanted to follow career-wise and he was now the youngest principal at the local Christian school. Glancing to his right, he saw his beautiful bride, Amelia. It had been a challenging ten years for them, both committed to honoring their beliefs and having friends thinking the worst, but as he told her, it really only mattered to them and God, no one else. While he was a bit nervous about the night ahead, he knew they would have fun figuring things out and he was grateful that his dad had been the role model he was to him.

He heard, "Bubba? Bubba come dance with me!" and felt a tug on his sleeve. Looking over, he saw Cailyn, now fourteen, standing there. "Come dance, Bubba! They're playing our song!" He tuned into what was playing and burst out laughing. "We Are Family" was blaring, their "family song" and he grinned all the way to the dance floor, even as Jonas pulled Amelia up to get her out there, telling her that she was now part of the family so she was required to dance.

***

Later that night, much, much later, he padded into the kitchen for something to drink, grateful that they had chosen to come to the cabin for a few days. Grabbing his phone, he sent off a text to his dad that simply said, "Thanks, Dad, for teaching me about being a man. I'm glad we waited. Love you, Thad."

About the Author

Darlene is a transplanted Yankee, moving from upstate New York when she was a teenager. She lives with the brat-cat pack and a small muffin dog, all rescues, as she plots and plans who will get to "talk" next!

Find me on Facebook!

https://www.facebook.com/darlenetallmanauthor

Want to read my first book, "Bountiful Harvest"? You can get it here:

http://mybook.to/BountifulHarvest

And my second book, "His Firefly", which released 11/3/16:

http://myBook.to/HisFirefly

And my third book, "His Christmas Pixie", which released 11/30/16:

http://myBook.to/HisChristmasPixie

Printed in Great Britain
by Amazon